The Jesus Horse

Melinda West Seifert

The Jesus Horse

"The job which the writer is doing

is to tell you a moving story

of the human heart in conflict."

~ William Faulkner

This is such a story.

ISBN-13:
978-0615955735 (Melinda West Seifert)

ISBN-10:
0615955738

The Jesus Horse is a trademark of Melinda West Seifert.

This book is a work of fiction. Names, characters and incidents either are the product of the author's imagination or are used fictitiously, and any resemblance to actual persons, living or dead, businesses, companies, events, or locales is entirely coincidental.

The publisher and the author of this book are not responsible for any products and services mentioned or referred to in this book, and disclaim any liability regarding the information offered in this book. They also disclaim any responsibility for any damage, loss, or expense to property arising out of, or relating to, the text in this book.

Manufactured in the United States of America. (November 2014)

First Edition

For my family. I love you dearly. Each and every one.

The Jesus Horse

Narrator

July 2011

Is it that we all need to believe in something? Is it a hunger for ultimate salvation, or simply a magnificent quest, one in search of whatever it is we spend our lives pursuing? Can those needs, or dreams or pursuits ever be met, and by what—a mission, a vision, a delusion, a higher power, something else, or maybe from somewhere deep within ourselves, maybe a place we have never even stumbled upon. Who knows? Maybe all we really want is a happy ending.

In part, this is a story about a horse, about the life, the time, in a way, the very being of an amazing, maybe miraculous horse, sort of *The Jesus* of horses. Not as irreverent as it might at first sound, it's just the way it is. It is in fact, exactly what it is.

But there's more. This is also a story about temptation, betrayal, loss, hope, faith, success, triumph and redemption. It's a story of people with stories, people of despair and people with the capacity for great joy. It's a story of now, a story of today and each day, and at the same time, a story of a time that has never been, or perhaps, a time that has already been. That pretty much sums life, and this story, up. Yes, that's a lot.

And, who am I you might wonder, to offer reason or explanation, to even begin to justify those parts of our hearts and souls that build the bridges we share with each other?

My qualifications are the same as yours. We are all a part of the dramas we create and live, we draw others in and they become a part of ours just as we are drawn in and become a part of theirs. It's as if there is an underground river, running through our lives and relationships, hollowing out beds in the sediment, sending us the very messages that shape our perceptions, judgments, and our own ideas of self and others. This tributary is as natural as the blood running through our bodies. In that we are all the same.

All told, I'm really just a very ordinary person, from a pretty ordinary background, who's lived a somewhat ordinary life. Dad worked the same job from college graduation to retirement. He had a family to support and there was no room to make a reality of dreams of greater goals. Mother taught school to help make ends meet. My husband and I too, struggle to make ends meet. We struggled to get our daughters through college. We continue to struggle with what we have made our "life's work." But, struggle is not all bad. It has its merits. In this, I may or may not be a lot like you—but there is one special thing about me. I have a very, very special horse.

Part One

April 1997

Pre-dawn, Sunday morning. The stars were still brilliant, but resting, fading, in that early morning stage of what remained of their lit-up, glittering, glory. The grey mare had been on her side, legs fully extended, for 10 minutes. Her allantoic membrane had already broken and the allantoic fluid that would lubricate the birth canal had been released. Strong contractions of the abdominal and uterine muscles irritated her. She had been up and down six times, kicking at her belly, biting her sides and stamping her back feet.

One stall over two bay mares stood together, heads over the rails, watching the birth. They would foal soon themselves, not for the first time, and were already familiar with the process. But, this was the grey mare's first foal, and she wasn't at all sure what was happening. And, she couldn't do anything but let it happen.

As she again lay in the bed of straw, experiencing one of the strongest contractions yet, something else began to happen. First the amniotic membrane, then the foal's forelegs, head tucked between them, then its shoulders and finally its hips made their appearance. Both the mare and foal rested, with the foal's hind legs still in the mare. After a few minutes the mare stood up, expelling the hind legs and breaking the navel cord. The new foal continued to rest in the straw bed while the last contractions finally delivered the mare's placenta.

The foal had been early. The timing had been miscalculated and signs that the mare was soon to foal had been missed. Neither the vet nor the foreman nor the owners had been present for the birth. Witnessed only by other horses the event went off without a hitch, much like 90 percent of all equine births.

The stars were quiet, dawn came, and with it an almost blood red sky. Streaks of purple punctuated the atmosphere, the striations like arched eyebrows over quizzical eyes, looking down at the world, and more specifically, the barn at Wildmare Farms.

The sky changed from red and purple to tangerine, then to lilac and then to an early morning blue. It became a buttermilk sky filled with soft cream-puff clouds, and the sun burst through them in great, long rays, down to the trees, creating a shimmering sprinkle of dew diamonds that sparkled on the leaves with a fresh but too short-lived brilliance.

Mia didn't have to get up early to feed. That was why they'd finally hired a foreman, who had in turn hired the hands whose job it was to care for the barns and of course, as her husband Richard put it, the "extravagantly overpriced Arabians" who lived comfortably in the barns. There were 28 horses in all; 18 mares, three stallions standing at stud, four new foals and three geldings. Now there were 29, but no one knew that yet.

Cleaning stalls, feeding and checking on the general condition of each horse took about three hours out of every morning. Exercise and training took another five to six hours of the day. If there were any breedings scheduled, that would be another two to three hours. And this was just the part of the ranch that revolved around the horses. This was the part of the ranch that Mia cared about, as well as the part her husband felt was a Texas-size sink hole down which they did nothing all day long but pour money.

But, Mia was up earlier than usual on this particular Sunday morning. She and Richard had argued long and late the night before. They argued about the horses, the money it took to maintain the stock and the barns and Richard, as always, kept coming back to, "where are all the sales, where is all the profit, why are we doing what we're doing?"

She had pointed out that there had been and continued to be sales, just not that many, yet. It took longer than six years to make a go of a high-quality breeding operation. Breeding Crabbet Arabians was not an expensive hobby as Richard put it. To Mia it was a business and a passion, in no particular order. It was the same.

Some of her horses descended from Arabians bred at Crabbet Park Stud in England, whose foundation horses were selected directly from the Arabian desert by the Stud's founders, Lady Anne and Wilfrid Blunt. In 1878 the Blunts traveled to the mid-east desert to obtain the best Arabian horses available. The pedigree of each horse was authenticated by the Bedoins and included historic accounts of the horses' heroic loyalty during tribal desert battles and wars. Later, select Crabbet-bred horses were bred to pure Egyptian bloodlines resulting in stock that highlighted the Arabians' leading character traits of loyalty and devotion while enhancing size, strength and stamina. The result—dry, fine, elegance.

The quality Mia loved most and worked hardest to foster was the breed's unique temperament, its reputation as a "people-lover." It was as if the horses had the magical power to possess their owners, enabling them to extract from their owners the same loyalty and dedication they so generously gave.

Until 1970 when it was dispersed, the Stud breeding program influenced the quality of Arabian horses bred worldwide. It still did through small breeding programs scattered throughout the world. It was programs like these that Mia hoped to emulate. And, it wasn't that she had grandiose ideas to improve the entire breed, she wanted to improve individual animals within specific pedigree limits. It wasn't a complicated concept and she really didn't understand why Richard had not only lost interest, but seemed combative over the whole process.

Actually, in a hidden truth, Mia knew well enough and deep down, but could not or would not verbalize it, that the arguments went deeper than the ranch. They were arguments of the soul, and they were slowly but surely sucking the joy from her dream.

It had been her money, her inheritance, her idea and her vision. It had also been her decision, although she had wanted Richard's approval and involvement, which he had willingly, mostly, given. He'd had lots of the why this won't work arguments, and she had countered every one of them. It was when she presented the entire operation to him as an adventure that his attitude swiftly changed.

When defined as a venture worthy of gamble and risk, words that appealed to Richard's daredevil, expansive self-perception, he seemed excited about the prospect of owning and running a ranch and breeding operation. But that was just it, it had been the idea of it, the persona of who he could be.

He'd bought the hat, boots and boot-cut jeans. He'd learned to ride, after a fashion, and one of the ranch hands was teaching him to rope. He'd been almost, at least from appearances, as involved in the process as she was. But with Richard, a former stockbroker and day trader, the excitement had worn off, and it had worn off quickly. Now it was just another job, one he seemed to no longer want, one that was hot and a lot of work, and it was true, one that so far wasn't paying off. But it would.

The thing about Richard, from the start, at least the thing that had probably first attracted Mia to him, was that he was a bit of a rogue. In a good way. Really a lovable way. Mia never knew what to expect. Sometimes it was a pleasant surprise, sometimes it was an unpleasant shock. More often than not it was a bolt from the blue.

Richard was streetwise. He was full of practical knowledge and information. In a rough hewn way, he was handsome. He had a surprisingly astute , internalized code of honor, which was one of the things Mia loved most about him. It served as a confirmation of sorts that he was, for all his shortcomings, a good person. It wasn't a stretch to acknowledge that Richard was a highly individualistic and self-reliant personality.

Lost in her own thoughts, Mia opened the doors to the mares' barn. She breathed deeply of the warm smells of fresh spring first-cut hay, manure and horse. They were scents she loved. It was 7am, and no one had even begun the morning feedings. Nickers greeted her and soft, whiskered muzzles appeared over stall gates.

The stalls in this barn had been designed to accommodate a mare and new foal. Each box stall was 12 x 12 with removable partitions on one side so a double stall could be created for the foaling and nursing mares. It was in the third stall on the right of the aisle that Mia stopped to talk to the grey mare, her favorite in those moments she dared admit it.

She had been particular about the breeding of this mare, whose Egyptian bloodlines went back to Hanan and her offspring, Jamil, a U.S. National Top Ten stallion. Crabbet bloodlines went back to Dajanieh, one of the Stud's best-known production mares and its pure white stallion, Mirage. Improving the breeding stock was one of the huge costs Richard didn't seem to appreciate. And yet it was critical to the success of the entire operation.

The grey mare greeted her with an affectionate nicker, but then turned away toward the back of the stall. This was not normal behavior from this horse. Mia opened the stall gate, and there was the foal, already standing awkwardly on legs almost as long as its mother's. The foal was dry now and appeared at first glance to be a chestnut filly.

Mia approached the foal slowly, not wanting to startle it or the mare. When it turned toward her, it looked straight at her, as if it already knew her. She felt an immediate, sharp and electric connection and that was when she saw the star.

Outlined by the reddish-brown chestnut, first foal coat, it was white, an almost perfect star shape, but a star with a tail that trailed down the foal's nose. It's a shooting star, thought Mia. She had been prepared to name the foal from its lineage, but now, her mind was working out a new pattern. The unexpected birth, the beautiful, bright Sunday morning, now full of hope, and the shooting star marking. Estrella de Dominga. Milagro de la Estrella de Dominga. Estrella. The words, the name, seemed to roll through her and dance out of her mouth. Sunday Star Miracle. It was perfect.

The foal watched Mia carefully. Its mother was close by and didn't seem to be at all concerned by the intrusion of this person thing. The person was moving forward, making soft noises. Ears flicked forward, the grey mare allowed Mia to approach. Stroking the mare's neck, she reached around and lightly, gently, and so slowly as to not appear to move at all, touched the foal. The touch continued and became light, lingering strokes, the soft noises continued, and the foal was content.

That was Sunday. By Wednesday the mare and foal were turned out to pasture together. Estrella, the more comfortable shortened version of the name Mia had settled on, or Stella as she had already nicknamed her, explored everything. Of the Wildmare foals over the last two years, Mia had never seen a foal quite like this one. It was about much more than curiosity, Stella seemed to have an innate understanding, an almost out of place sense of the world around her. It was as if everything was instinctive, already programmed into who she was.

Even at her young age, if Stella could speak the language of the humans there were so many things she would say. There was little of what the world was about that these human people creatures understood. How could it be like this for them? They went about their individual business, always in search of something. Was it redemption, a revelation, maybe just simple gratification? But to Stella, these people had it all wrong. As far as she could see, they placed their needy, aggressive, sometimes hostile and almost entirely emotional demands, far too far above their more basic needs, which it seemed to her, should be the first and main concern.

And they spent so much time in the past, or maybe it was in the future. Didn't they understand about now? Didn't they see the past for what it was? It couldn't love them, or nurture them, or even communicate with them. Didn't they know that the past is already an abandoned place, a place maybe never quite lost, but at the same time, a place that can never be again? And as for the future, it would be here soon enough, but it too, was not a place to be. Not yet. Now, well, now was here, and it was all there really was that was of any substance—rational, physical or tangible. Why wasn't there more emphasis on now? It was the only thing that could be at all controlled, and wasn't that what these people were after? Control?

Stella understood such things, but communicating her thoughts was something else entirely. How? And, to whom?

It was all about time and space. You move toward one every bit as surely as you move away from another. Stella knew both were merely a matter of perspective. Already, she had bridged the two. Now it was time to begin making the connections. She was just a baby, but her soul was an old soul. And the answers to all the unasked, unknown questions, were there, in her soul. Waiting. Stella knew, but Stella couldn't tell.

Each new image for the foal was more like a creation, a birth in itself, certainly a discovery, but all still too new to be a memory. Yet Stella, at the age of three days, already understood quite well both the injustice, and fairness of the world, and even more than that, that each had the potential to be more violent, or beautiful than the next, taking its toll and marking time. She understood that through it all there would be at the same time and with the same intensity, the potential for the greatest of joys to bring and hold it all together, or the greatest of tragedy to tear it just as quickly down.

Stella was a gentle foal. The rhythm of her heart was a gentle rhythm. She had accepted the halter with little resistance. She allowed herself to be led both nearside and offside. With a little encouragement and a lot of patience, she allowed her feet and legs to be lifted and held for short periods.

She loved to play and had a natural teasing and mischievous nature. Galloping around the grey mare was a good game. Stella would gallop in first small, then larger circles around her mother, then come to an abrupt stop to see if she had been noticed. By the time she was 10 weeks old, there were new foals to play with, and the grey mare was no longer her only source of entertainment or security.

It was when Stella appeared to be resting or sleeping, a natural activity for a foal, that she was actually developing along another, unrecognizable and hidden path, one that was to shape far more than her own life. These were the times she spent thinking, connecting and understanding the complexities, patterns and limitations of the world she had become a part of.

With life moving at a steady pace, Stella's development and behavior from all outward signs, indicated the makings of an easy-going and eager-to-please horse. Mia assumed it was all in the genes, what was meant by "breeding will tell." She loved the little foal, but she loved all the foals. Still, there was something about Stella that was different, polls apart different, from the others. Something special, probably even extraordinary, but also something more than a little unsettling.

There was indeed, something about Stella. In many ways by the time she was two and a half months old she was as mature as most of the adult mares. She still had her playful, willful, stubborn side, but there was none of the foal skittishness that took so much effort and work to bring under control. Stella, herself, was already in control.

Mia considered it her job, as well as her privilege to work with the foals. They were the future, of the farm as well as her own livelihood. To a greater extent, she saw them as the future of the breed. They were the young, they would become the new stallions and mares, they would become the champions and they would carry on the line, and then they would become the old. Such was the timeline of life. Sure, it was overstating and more than a little pretentious on her part, but on a large scale it was true. Each breeding operation like hers would either turn out well-developed, well-mannered and well-bred horses, or it would just turn out more horses. And that was one of the inherent problems with breeding Arabians. There were too many "just horses."

Stella was not "just a horse." She was smart. She was opinionated, she was at the same time both willful and willing, she was certainly beautiful, she was well-boned and classically built, and she had those double swirls on her forehead.

Mia had studied swirls and patterns, and their interpretation. She knew swirls had been used to predict characteristics in horses for over three hundred years. Most horses have a single swirl pattern in the hair, usually between or just above the eyes. It's said a single swirl means a generally uncomplicated horse. Horses with a single swirl several inches below the eyes are said to be creative, imaginative and intelligent, often amusing themselves at the expense of their owners by untying lead ropes, opening latches and turning on water valves.

Then there are horses, such as Stella, with two swirls, adjoining one above the other or side by side, above, below or between the eyes. Horse lore says horses with these double swirls tend to be more emotional, more intelligent, more intent on doing things their way, and more over-reactive to the environment around them. That was Stella.

Another thing about Stella, although it never occurred to Mia that it was actually Stella, was that when Mia was around her, the oddest thoughts seemed to just pop into her head. Not really pop so much as explode, march in and invade. Divide and conquer? Deep, intensely private thoughts that seemed to come from nowhere, thoughts Mia would never in a lifetime of untold years have come up with on her own, thoughts that just all of a sudden were, and would suddenly take control. And the worst part, or maybe the best part was, they made sense. In some really different and inexplicable way, they made all the sense in the world. Except Mia didn't know what to make of them. As far as she knew, they were not her thoughts, yet they ended up in her head all the same.

Only the week before, she had been grooming Stella, lifting and holding her feet, rubbing her gums, gently massaging her ears, doing all the right things to get a foal used to human handling, all the while, the latest argument with Richard playing like a closed loop throughout her mind. The loop had been abruptly interrupted with a new thought, much the way a newscaster would cut into a program with breaking, life-altering, earth-shattering news.

"It's about his sense of usefulness. Actually, there is none. It's been lost and has now been replaced with false circumstances, and now he's made them real. But make no mistake, he's not an innocent victim. He's created the role he plays, he's made it his own, and now he wants you to embrace it too. A change of heart changes everything."

Where that came from, Mia had no idea. She had never been a deep thinker, more a person content with life as it presented itself and making of it what she could. "A change of heart? Exactly whose heart? Exactly what change?"

Then, just a few days later, still more.

"Life and its realities have room to bend a little, stretch a little, even warp a bit, but not the truth of it. The truth of it never changes at all."

Too much, too many ambiguous answers to even more ambiguous questions. Mia had the idea that something important had happened, but couldn't even begin to guess at what it was. It was as if she had been challenged to see but not told what to look for. Maybe, probably, it was absurd to try. Without a question, how was she going to find an answer?

When the answer came, it came not so much as a surprise but more as a confirmation of all that was wrong with the world, at least with her world.

Richard had been withdrawn, even more withdrawn and moody than usual. He was making more trips into town than was typical, at least for him. He hadn't asked the usual Richard questions, and that was the first indication things were heading south, though Mia hadn't yet made that connection. To top it off, he hadn't shown any interest in training or sales. Richard had always been keenly interested in sales. Something wasn't right. Mia had finally asked, bluntly, just where it was exactly that he was going every day? That brought it to a head when Richard responded that he was busy working on projects in town. Projects of his own. Important projects.

"I have a life too, you know. I still have skills and abilities that other people value. You have your little projects, I have mine."

Great, thought Mia. Just what I need. Richard with more attitude than usual. She'd tried to get him to open up, to include her in what he was doing, but no luck. Whatever Richard was doing, he was intent on doing it without her. It was that he didn't want to include her that hurt.

Feeling shutout, brought back memories of the past, some of it a happy past, much of it lonely. As a child Mia had been what people called horse-crazy, wanting to spend every minute at a barn or stable, any barn or stable. In those powerful, perfectly designed and gentle creatures she saw an almost impossible mix of gracefulness and fragility, size, strength and intelligence. From picture book horses, to stuffed toy horses, to model horses to her first encounter with a real, living, breathing animal, they immediately took hold of a timeless, designated place in her heart. That place was more solid now than ever.

School dances, sleepovers, boys, or any other distraction, didn't even come close to horses. Maybe that had been the problem when it came to making and maintaining friendships. Mia had been on plenty of dates, usually doubling with other couples, but had never had a serious boyfriend until Richard, and by then, he was working as a stockbroker and she was a senior in college.

She knew people viewed her as stuck-up and unapproachable. Yet, that's not at all how she saw herself. She would have liked friends, invitations, to be included. She just hadn't known how to put herself out there for others to choose or shun. Some life for a pretty girl. Some life for anyone. Yet, she had been very content in her world, even happy. Where had that truly, blissful, innocent happiness gone, she sometimes wondered?

Richard had been different. He had appealed to that side of Mia that had always been a little unconventional. The side that told her to go for what she knew she wanted, whether it was a popular, sensible choice or not. Richard had held an element of excitement that Mia's life had been missing, and when he had asked her to marry him, it seemed as if the puzzle pieces, after such a long time, were finally falling into the place they belonged.

But then, the thing about puzzles, they fit until they don't. Drop them, and you start over.

It hadn't taken very long for Mia to find out what Richard was really up to in town. His project's name was Gretchen.

Richard's spin on Gretchen was that she was the first of many new clients. He was helping her with her portfolio. Out with the old, in with the new. Some stock just wasn't worth holding on to. Surely Mia could understand that. Yes, she understood.

A month later, Mia walked into the bedroom to find Richard packing.

"Business?"

"I'm leaving."

"On business? When will you be back?"

"I won't be back. I'm leaving. I know it seems sudden, but I think it's best this way. I'm not happy here, you're not happy with me, and we don't seem to be happy together. I need to find something in my life that's worthwhile, while I still can. This whole place is dragging me down, and if you're willing to go down with it, that's your choice, but it's not mine."

"Count," thought Mia to herself. "One, two, three, four, five. Now breathe."

"So, I'm leaving."

And he did. He left. Just like that. Flat out gone. Oh, he said goodbye on his way out the door. Mia had something to say to him as well. She didn't know where the words came from, they were hers, and they weren't, but it didn't really matter. She had her say and he was gone all the same.

Good, bad, better, worse, she couldn't say. But, she was alone, and she knew immediately, without a doubt, it was a hard place to be.

As complicated as her situation was becoming, in some ways, Mia felt what might be a sense of relief, at least a reprieve from daily battle with Richard. The arguments would stop. She would make the decisions and choices that would determine her success or failure, and she didn't consider failure an option. Richard could no longer hold her back, and she saw that, all on its own, as a way to move forward. She was also moving forward with what felt like a huge hole, a hollow, hurtful place in her heart.

What concerned her was why. Why had Richard left? Why had he left her?

Mia knew only one thing had changed. Richard was gone, out of her life, and she was pretty sure he was gone for good. But in that act, everything changed. The way she felt about herself, her life up to now, certainly the way she felt about Richard, and maybe even harder to face, what was she to make of the future. Was it her? What had she done? What hadn't she done? What had Richard done that had nothing to do with her?

She knew the real reasons, whatever they were, weren't even the issue. They didn't really matter, not in the long stretch ahead. Now, it was just time to let go. It was time to release Richard into his own life. It was on him now to see where it would go.

Still, she felt his betrayal with a razor-sharp intensity as surely as if she had been cleanly, brutally cut, and then, cut-off. There was a physical pain to match the mental one. It ripped through her, leaving a long, jagged and open scar in its path. And more. More than she could define.

In her mind, the matter of Richard's unfaithfulness, no matter how she tried to bring it around to where it made some sort of sense, remained an unresolved disappointment. Quietly screaming inside, Mia knew no sound had escaped. The crash and its echo were trapped in her throat, her chest, her lungs, her being, trying to shatter it seemed, what was left of the sense of self-confidence she had worked hard to build. What she was left with was emptiness, loss, grief, anger and debt. A great deal of each.

There were too many why questions, and too few answers, and Mia knew the answers were false. There was no reason she could imagine that would ease her sorrow. She was mourning, but she wasn't sure for whom or why. Everything had changed, yet she was the same.

Still, she had the horses. If she had a future at all it was in the horses, and without a doubt, that future was here and now, looming and intimidating, and at the same time, unavoidable.

Rubbing Stella down Mia talked non-stop. Why she was telling this horse her problems she didn't know. But she had to tell someone before the anger and hurt consumed her, and Stella was a good listener.

Brushing and rubbing was a workout. It was cathartic, it was invigorating and in that, it was therapeutic, not to the point of liberating her from her grief, but maybe a way to move forward and a little away from it. It helped her feel normal again. Mia stopped to take a deep breath. She shook her head, to clear out the horse hair and dust as much as trying to clear her brain of the clatter Richard had left behind.

"So, move on. You have the choice to leave the past and make a new future. Richard faced temptation, everyone does, but he wasn't strong enough to resist. He looked for and found the easy way. And that won't last. Easy isn't really easy.

"If you go through life, leaving out, avoiding all the bad pieces, think about how simple it would be to go around tempting others with just the good and accepted parts of human behavior. That's not real life. Richard was tempted. And, that becomes Richard's problem and Richard's shortcoming. Don't make it yours."

Maybe Mia shouldn't have shaken her head with such force. Something was obviously loose. Or maybe this was what a psychotic break was like. She very slowly and as inconspicuously as possible looked around for the source of what she was hearing.

"Goodness doesn't just happen. It's not independent. It's not even autonomous. It doesn't develop outside of us, from the top down. Goodness grows from our strengths, whatever they are for each of us, and it grows from the bottom up, from the inside out. Believe it, we all want the same things. Immediate answers to our prayers, safety for our children and loved ones, cures for disease, and we want it all neatly tied up without ambiguity. We want it the way we want it. It's all the

same, we're all of us looking for some sort of redemption. And we're almost all looking in the wrong place.

"Anyone can face risk when there's no real danger. That's the easy part. And without the prospect of rejection, or a dangerous choice, it's easy to enjoy our luck, destinies, power and fortune. But, to what end?"

Mia looked at Stella, who was looking intently back at her. Stella's expressive eyes seemed to speak to her soul.

"Only love can bring about a response of love, and love grows slowly along a twisted, winding path. It takes its time. It makes its place. Love has its own power, a power that like goodness grows from within, and it is only this that can conquer the human heart. This is not Richard's world. He hasn't yet learned that love, like hate, is powerless if the beloved chooses to reject it."

Mia didn't know if she was hallucinating, sleepwalking, completely losing it, or something more. She knew though that whatever it was she was clinging to could all dissolve more quickly than the blink of an eye, as if it had never been, and could never be again. She had to hold on. To something. And, maybe this was it, maybe it was all there was. Maybe it meant clinging to the past, which would at some point lead inevitably to the future. But for now, there was nothing it seemed left to lose, and at the same time, nothing to choose in its place.

"You'll find your way. There's an exact moment for each of us when it's time to become your own hero. Sometimes, that's what you need most, and for you, that time is now."

October 1999

It's not that it was a particularly nasty divorce. As divorces go it was rather civilized. Richard moved out. Time passed. At first, Mia had wondered if he would be back, if things would change, but over time, she realized she no longer cared. In his own, inimitable way, Richard simply announced he didn't want to be married any longer. This wasn't the life he wanted, although he wasn't sure just what that was either. He had been very clear. It wasn't actually Mia, it was him, his shortcoming, his need to move on. He didn't know where.

Maybe it went back to his childhood and upbringing, or lack of upbringing. Maybe it had something to do with being an only child. Maybe he was afraid of failure, or success, or of being disappointed. Maybe he was afraid he would be swallowed by Mia's drive and quest for perfection. Yes, she would admit to that, but she had always thought of Richard as a partner as much as her husband.

One month after the divorce was final Richard remarried. His new wife, the Gretchen project, with whom it turned out he had been on intimate terms for almost three years, was a Realtor. She was 32 years old. She had been married once before and divorced well. She hated, and was deathly afraid of, horses. The happy couple moved to San Francisco where Richard just knew he would find what he was missing in life.

Mia didn't have a clue where her life was now heading. She was exhausted. She felt she had accomplished nothing. The risk, the effort, the betrayal and defeat had all led her to this end, and now that it was ending, what of it was left? To what exactly did she have left to hold on to? A little money when all was said and done, very little when one considered where it had all started and what it had ultimately cost her. But now it wasn't about counting her gains or losses, now it was up to her to exploit what remained. Both picking up where she left off and moving forward from where she was at this specific point in time seemed suddenly to be foreign concepts to her. She didn't know how to begin.

She did know, however, on some level she had trouble even acknowledging, that if she was looking for anything like transcendent meaning in a universe of disappointment, disillusion and anguish, she was going to have to rediscover the traces of a humanity she had once believed in and that still surely existed somewhere, and make them her own. And she was going to have to do it at warp speed.

Throughout the divorce proceedings Mia had tried to see things from Richard's perspective. She wasn't at all sure why that was important to her or why she bothered. Wasn't she the injured party?

Wrapped in anger and hurt, it hadn't been easy. Dividing assets. Richard had at least been fair about the farm and horses, but it had been his income too that had gone into the day-in day-out operation.

The liquid cash account was no longer liquid. The value was in the farm and horses and the judge ruled part of it belonged to Richard. Richard was only interested in his share of cash. The split meant selling assets and to satisfy both Richard and the court, it meant Mia would lose what was now the most important part of her life. There was no other way but to sell the farm. Maybe she could find a smaller, more manageable place with her share of the proceeds?

It meant too, that she would have to sell some of her horses. She would have to literally start over. And, starting over wasn't something she looked forward to. She didn't see how that could even begin to smother the throbbing heartache that had become her life.

Unfortunately for all involved, both the real estate and horse market were down. Mostly down and out. To sell what she had built would be giving it away. That was assuming she could find a buyer, which so far wasn't happening. No offers, no interest, and certainly nothing that would satisfy Richard. And, nothing that would satisfy the amount the court said Richard was due. She was out of cash, out of time, and as far as she could see, out of options. She was out of hope. She was totally at a loss when it came to what was next.

Stella was becoming a fine horse. She was a beautiful animal, sharp, alert ears, just the right dish to her face and a noble expression that bordered on sad. But it was in her dark, wide-set eyes that something just out of reach lurked.

The grey mare, Stella's mother, remained Mia's favorite horse. More so now because of Mia's strong but conflicted feelings for Stella. While she loved and was completely comfortable with the grey mare, Stella, if the truth were told, scared her. She wasn't sure what to make of her.

It's not that Stella had ever actually done anything to frighten her. She was well-mannered, gentle, inquisitive and mostly calm. Mia just felt uncomfortable around her, a little afraid of who she was, yet at the same time, was drawn to be around her, felt a need to be around her.

She looked forward to the time she spent working with her, as with all the horses, but she knew the time she spent with Stella was somehow different. It was all at once, intense, exhausting and exhilarating. And, something more.

Mia had gotten into the habit of spending several hours with the horses before bed. She would turn on all the lights in the main barn and go from horse to horse, trying to divide her time between them. When she allowed herself to be honest, she knew there wouldn't be much more time to spend with them. It was soothing, almost encouraging to be around the horses. She felt as if she could draw her own sorely needed strength from their great, massive power.

And, little by little, her betrayal, anger and grief were giving way to a new outlook. She couldn't define it, but somehow the rawness of Richard's betrayal didn't seem quite so raw. She was beginning to wonder if betrayal was even the right emotion. Maybe it was more about choices. And, she well knew, every choice has a consequence.

It was Christmas Eve on one such night. Mia was spending Christmas alone. It was what she wanted.

She had strung strands of colored lights around the rafters in the barn, and had outlined the roofline with lights. It wasn't much, and she wasn't much in the mood for Christmas, but it was in making the effort to celebrate the season that she felt the first, small, glimmer of hope. Just a flicker, but it was a start.

She stopped in Stella's stall and gently ran her hands over the horse's well-muscled body.

"We're all of a piece, our existence. We move between instants, some without time or memory, some without hope or disappointment. They just are. Others tear us down. Others dance. Others take us where we want to go. We're all going somewhere, you know. The questions are, where? Why? And, how will we get there? It's our own part in the plan that provides the answers. It's how we participate that makes all the difference."

Well, there it was. Mia knew by now that Stella had something to do with what she had come to think of as "her awakening." She didn't know how and she didn't know exactly what, but whatever it was, it was happening, and it happened when she was around Stella. It scared the hell out of her and fascinated her all at the same time. And, it was beginning to inspire her, just a little. She was almost allowing herself to believe the faint glimmer of light wasn't an earth-bound meteor with her coordinates in its site after all, but perhaps, maybe, a star of hope.

She was beginning to believe more in herself, and that she could and would face head-on what she had to face. Perhaps this was what was meant by faith?

January 2000

Bankruptcy. Mia hated the word. She knew it was just a legal term, a way to protect what little she could scrape together and still be as fair as she could to the creditors. She hated most what it stood for. Failure. And, loss. The loss of everything she loved. Her life had indeed become a quiet desperation. At the same time, it was a place she didn't know how to leave.

Richard was already lost, but he had been gone in spirit a long time. His had been a departure of will. She had already grieved for that loss, and the anger she felt at his unfaithfulness more than made up for the loss of his love. Now, she was letting the anger go. So far, its replacement was emptiness.

It was saying goodbye to the horses and Wildmare Farms that was slowly eating away at her soul. She wondered how long it would be before there was nothing left of her.

She had wanted to dispose of the horses herself, to sell them to reputable breeders with suitable barns, but the entire horse industry was depressed, the market for Arabians was almost non-existent, buyers were few and the court had ordered all holdings to be sold at auction. Her horses—reduced to such a cold word as "holdings." All of the horses. She wasn't to keep a single horse. What would she do with a horse now anyway? Soon she wouldn't even have a home.

Bankruptcy hadn't been Mia's choice. She would have preferred time to find a way to work things out, with the bank, her creditors and Richard. But Richard, and the creditors were impatient. Chapter 7 was an involuntary bankruptcy, what they explained as a straight bankruptcy. In one of the most patronizing tones she had ever heard, the attorney had explained that when all was liquidated, she would have a fresh start, free from creditors and the pressures of overwhelming debt. "Didn't that sound nice? She would actually come out on top, without future obligation on those discharged debts."

"What a total ass," Mia had thought. How could anyone be so obtuse and thick as to not understand what she was going through, offering false platitudes to paint a picture that could never be.

If she had been able to keep up the mortgage payments on the farm and house, she could have kept at least that, but without the horses, who had to be sold, there was no income, so, no mortgage payment, so in short, goodbye everything.

Everything she owned down to the last manure fork had been inventoried. The horses had been appraised based on age, lineage and degree of training. Mia knew none would sell for close to the appraised value, which was insultingly low to begin with.

There were 35 saddles, 10 show saddles, 48 saddle blankets, 46 cooling blankets, 48 winter blankets, 35 headstalls, 28 training bits, 30 riding bits, 26 show bits, and miscellaneous lead ropes and halters and training cavesons. Then there was the farm equipment, tractors, trailers and trucks. There was of course the real estate; house, stables, sheds and storage buildings, all on 150 rolling, cultivated acres.

Mia figured $189,000 if she were lucky enough to get an average of $4,500 for each horse, horses for which she had paid on average more than four times that amount. The farm had appraised for $1.2 million. She had a mortgage of $750,000, which would only leave a profit of $450,000, assuming it sold anywhere near the appraised value. Good luck getting that price.

All the farm equipment had only come to $72,000. And used tack sold at auction for next to nothing. Mia figured maybe $11,000 tops. Add it all up and if all went at the appraised values, the auction and real estate sale could bring $722,000 after the mortgage was paid.

By the time she paid back salaries, lawyers, credit card debt, and all other accounts, which totaled close to $600,000, that would leave $122,000 to split with Richard. And that would leave Mia with about $61,000 to start a new life. Not much to show for so much work, the loss of a marriage, and enough anger, hurt and grief to last the rest of several lifetimes. This all assumed of course that everything would sell at either Mia's estimated, or better still, the appraised value, and she knew it would not. It was entirely likely she could be left with absolutely nothing but unresolved, even if discharged, debt.

Amarillo, Texas

Mia had been in the business long enough to know what happened at auctions. They serve a purpose, but not always a good one. On the good side, the term "horse auction" conjures up images of whitewashed Kentucky and Virginia sales rings, where sleek and shiny yearling thoroughbreds are sold for tens of thousands to hundreds of thousands of dollars. But Mia knew there was a darker side to horse auctions.

All around the country, the local horse auction, commonly held at county livestock markets, is still the primary place where people buy and sell horses. Thousands of horses are auctioned each year, including healthy well-trained pleasure horses and ponies, racehorses that didn't make it at the track or at stud, stolen horses, old horses, sick horses, and donkeys and mules. Thousands of horses purchased at auctions are also slaughtered each year, bought for seventy-five to eighty cents per pound. For an 1100 pound horse, that's $880. Their meat is then sent overseas to Europe and Asia where it is sold on average for $15 to $20 a pound.

Active in Equine Advocates, a non-profit equine protection and horse rescue organization, Mia had seen undercover footage showing the brutal process of butchering horses for meat. She had seen the horses struggle in the chute, a bolt gun held to their heads. The bolt, shot into the skull, is supposed to split the skull rendering the horse unconscious before it is strung up to have its throat split. She could only imagine the horror in the horse's mind, hearing the shrill screams of other horses, slipping and sliding on blood-soaked floors trying to escape the unavoidable. The thought of it all turned Mia's stomach cold, clammy, and sick.

She knew some people at auctions were simply looking for bargains. Some were looking for inexpensive riding horses. She knew too, that far too many of the horses sold at local auctions were purchased by the slaughter buyers.

And because killer buyers are paid by the pound for the horses they deliver, they too look for healthy horses in good body condition, as well as horses in poor condition who can be fattened up with cheap feed.

Mia was in the horse business, or had been. She knew only too well the costs, and she knew that many people simply buy a horse, without thinking through ahead of time the responsibility, expense, or time involved in caring for horses.

Some owners don't understand a horse's specialized requirements, and many can't afford proper veterinary care. The winter months are particularly bad for neglected horses because they aren't generally able to graze on pasture. Many of those horses never have access to pasture. Denied necessary sustenance and in a weakened condition, these horses are often just loaded onto trailers and shipped off to auction for sale.

Didn't people realize where their pets were going? The sad thing was, the slaughter houses themselves were providing unknowing horse owners with an easy dumping ground instead of forcing them to take responsibility for their horses.

Breed, size, color, and temperament mean nothing to the killer buyer. Each of the horses was once a faithful friend of someone, or maybe the wild horse who slipped through the cracks, or unwanted or stolen horses; but the same fate awaited them all.

Even famous horses weren't spared. Mia had read about the 1986 Kentucky Derby winner Ferdinand, the big, beautiful chestnut son of Nijinsky II, whose bloodlines traced directly back to Northern Dancer. After winning the Derby, Ferdinand went on to take the 1987 Horse of the Year title in the Breeders Cup Classic with a dramatic victory over 1987 Derby hero, Alysheba. Ferdinand was "disposed" of in 2002 in a Japanese slaughter plant after he failed to be a productive stud.

Mia couldn't understand how as a society people didn't value their animals more than to discard them at will. What does that say about society as a whole? What does it say about life? What does it say about the privileged and underprivileged, the perfect and the imperfect? How do you measure a horse's usefulness or still, a person's worth, when they are no longer able to perform or manage? It was all about so much more.

The past does indeed become the present, and it does indeed determine the future. It was a question of humanity, and lately Mia wasn't too keen on the human race. It seemed as if all the pieces of the collective fabric that held her life together were unraveling. And, she couldn't find the loose thread to stop it.

The Amarillo Livestock Auction had a good reputation, but Mia knew the killer buyers would be there. Over the period of three days it would auction off approximately 300 horses. Some of those horses would be the result of bankruptcy sales. Some would be registered competition horses. Some would be family pets and ponies. Some would go to good homes and some were destined for the slaughter house.

The horses from Wildmare Farms were corralled mostly together, weaned foals in one pen, yearlings in another, mares in a nearby pen, and the stallions separated from the mares for everyone involved's sake. It was better than many auctions in that the best horses were placed in like lots.

Stella, now technically a three year-old, was in the same pen as her mother and 27 other horses. All of the horses were nervous, and Stella was no exception. There were no stalls, no covered shelter. It was a new and different experience and there was something about the upheaval of it all that gave it a sense of urgency, despair and finality, and perhaps, pending disaster.

The sky had threatened all day, but by evening, well before sunset, it had darkened, with an ominous, foreboding aura. Menacing thunderheads were building in anvil-shaped cumulonimbus clouds and the wind had picked up, blowing sand and caliche from the corrals with a stinging ferocity.

The air was heavy with humidity and anticipation. The rising, warmer air finally reached the level where the temperature was at dew point. Condensation grew and the water vapor became visible steam. It was at this point the sharply defined base of the first towering cumulous cloud began to form. The air continued to rush upward, rising about 2,000 feet a minute. Within three minutes, what had started on the surface was now a nautical mile high.

With height, as the air in the column cooled, water vapor condensed and formed water droplets which were carried upward. The cloud continued to grow in size while the amount of suspended water increased to the point the rising warm air could no longer hold it aloft. Because of the size of the cloud, and the clouds that had now formed around it, the water began to freeze as it began its descent, collecting more water, which in turn froze another layer of water. The ice formation in the clouds was key for turning the huge energy potential into a super storm cell.

The falling ice pellets, or graupel as the announcer on the 6:00 news liked to say and explain, over and over, were negatively charged. Small, supercooled cloud droplets that struck and bounced off the graupel became positively charged. Lightning.

Mia had checked her horses a final time before going back to the motel. She didn't have a say in what the next day would bring, but she would be there to see it. She would reconcile it, if only for herself, then.

By 10:00 pm, severe thunderstorm, severe weather, and flash flood warnings had been issued for most of Potter and Randall Counties. By 10:28 they were a reality.

The rain pounded the corralled horses in sheets. The dark sky wasn't dark long as lightning struck at a rate of over 60 strikes per minute. Anyone foolish, crazy or simply unfortunate enough to be out in the storm could actually hear, almost feel, the electrical impulses as the quarter-sized lightning bolts repeatedly struck the earth.

Most of the horses from Wildmare Farms had never been in a storm like this one. They were used to shelter at night, a roomy stall, thick bedding, and plenty of hay. The younger horses ran in frantic circles as best they could in the cramped corral. Some of the older horses, including the grey mare, milled together in the center of the corral. Stella stood quivering against the wood fencing, her body pressed as close to rotting rails as she could manage.

The slow-moving storm seemed in no hurry to move on. Every crack of thunder sent horses racing from side to side. Piercing and frantic whinnies competed with the deafening rain and thunder. The ground had turned to slick mud and silt, and several times horses lost their footing in their frantic race to escape, sliding and falling under other terror-stricken horses.

A series of lightning bolts, each considerably hotter than the surface of the sun, each carrying about 1 billion volts of power, shot as if aimed at the corral, one immediately after the other. The sky was lit with a screaming-hot electrified light. The thunder was almost simultaneous. And then, its damage done, the storm began to move off. Slowly, lessening in intensity. Steadily moving on to the north.

The smell of burning horses filled the air. Two horses lay dead in the center of the corral. It had only taken a quarter of a second for the strike. The four strikes that followed had only lasted a few ten thousandths of a second each. It had been more than enough to instantly kill the grey mare.

The new scents filled Stella's nostrils, and filled them with something she didn't understand. She moved toward the two horses. The other horses seemed to sense her puzzlement and concern, and moved away. As Stella approached, she nuzzled her mother to get her to rise. She didn't understand the lack of response. And then, she did.

Stella's sharp whinnies filled the air. Then she stood, head down, over her mother's body for the rest of the night.

That was how Mia found her horses the next morning, covered in mud, cuts, gashes, and blood.

Stella still had not left the grey mare. Mia had left a wakeup call for 5:00 a.m. Skipping breakfast, she wanted to get to the fairgrounds as early as possible, to check on her horses and spend as much time as possible with them. What she saw brought immediate sharp tears. Great sobs followed as she climbed through the fence rails, falling and sliding through the mud to get to Stella and the grey mare. She knew the mare was gone, but she couldn't believe it.

Mia felt her heart break, yet again. She knew the world was full of suffering, God, how she knew it. She was living it.

She knew too, that with all the human suffering, mourning a horse might seem a little eccentric, a little self-indulgent. But, Mia's feelings were nothing if not deeply human. To Mia, the grey mare had symbolized strength and beauty. She had been pure. How could anyone not grieve for the loss of such purity and grace?

Why this? Why now? Why these good horses? But the "why?" questions didn't seem to have answers.

"You can't answer the why questions. It's not the answers that are important. It's like asking why good people die and evil people live long, apparently successful lives. It's like asking why so many prayers seemingly go unanswered. It's about trust-in-spite-of."

Stella was still standing by the mare, next to where Mia knelt over the body, stroking the grey mare's graceful neck. When Mia looked up at her, she would remember for the rest of her life, that there were tears in Stella's sad eyes.

Activity at the stockyard was picking up as owners and employees appeared to assess and deal with the storm's damage. She knew it wouldn't be long before a backhoe would cart away the two carcasses. For Mia, it was a metaphor of her life. She had tried. She had tried to make a difference. In her heart, she felt she had failed miserably.

"You're not alone. It may feel that way now, but I promise, there are hundreds, thousands, even hundreds of thousands of people who feel as you do, people who want to make a difference, people who struggle to do the right thing. Just wait. Let in the light, keep it in your soul and in your heart. Don't give it up now. The greater your light, the brighter your world will be."

Stella was at it again.

Mia almost didn't turn around to acknowledge the voice behind her. Between the voices in her head and her grief she had lost her sense of place.

"Ma'am? Can I help? Let me help with these horses."

Mia looked at the man behind her. He was not much more than a boy, probably in his early twenties. What could he possibly do to help?

"My name's Zack. I've been looking at your horses since late yesterday. I'm sorry about your mares. I had my eye on that grey one."

"She was my favorite," said Mia. This is her daughter."

"My second choice. I'm going to try to bid her when the auction starts. They're all beautiful. I can only afford one horse. I hope it's her."

Zack reached a hand out to help Mia up.

Then he turned to Stella.

"Hey girl. So that's your mama. Poor girl. Poor baby. I lost my mama too. Maybe that gives us simpatico?"

Stella listened to the voice as if she was interested. Then the unmistakable diesel rumble announced the backhoes had arrived.

Wranglers began herding the horses to the far end of the corral to let the first backhoe in. Stella didn't want to move. Zack took a lead rope from one of the men and snapped it to her halter, then handed it to Mia.

"You hang on to her. I'll help get these horses loaded."

The first backhoe operator, a big, burly and not an especially happy looking man, Jim Bob, had already moved his equipment into place and was adjusting the bucket to push the grey mare out of the corral where she would be disposed of along with the other horses lost in the storm.

Before the operator could scoop up the grey mare's body, Zack intervened.

"This here lady's upset about her horses. Do it like this," said Zack, indicating the angle the operator should use to keep the grey mare's head from hanging out of the bucket, dragging along the ground.

The backhoe operator wasn't used to having someone he didn't work for tell him what to do, and ordinarily, it would have created a big problem, but looking at the scene in front of him, he felt the urge to cooperate. My God, he thought. I must be getting soft. But the idea of stepping back a bit, for once, didn't really bother him.

When the two horses had been removed Zack joined Mia and Stella. Taking the lead rope from Mia, he walked Stella around, noting her manners, movements and responses. As he ran his hands over her legs, neck, face, ears and back, Stella stood calmly, flicking her ears back and forth with curiosity.

For Mia it was all at once a great and good surprise to find a spirit of decency, heroism and maybe even hope in someone, especially in a person from whom you would never think to look for such ideals, a person you have never known and will in all likelihood, never know again. It was with that thought Stella interrupted.

"You see only what you look at. You want to see what you're looking for. They're more alike than you think."

As luck, or fate would have it, Mia's horses were the last lot and Stella was the last horse to be auctioned Saturday afternoon. Zack had waited, and for $2,500, he was the high bidder. With her breeding and bloodlines, Mia knew Stella should have brought at least five times that amount. Even given the current market for Arabians, $2,500 was well below the estimated price. It was also, unfortunately, in keeping with the other prices that had been realized.

At least it appeared that Stella was going to a new owner who appreciated her, would take care of her, and develop her potential. Her horses had escaped the killer buyers. Others had not been so lucky.

Mia watched as Zack loaded Stella into his old dented, mostly rusted trailer. He carefully tied her, filled the hay net with fresh hay and pulled the screen down over the window. Stella let out one last long whinny as they pulled away.

"The past is never lost. It's just another part of the journey, from season to season, from place to place, from the known to the unknown, from hope to new hope. Believe it, where you are now, your present situation, this is not your final destination."

It was as if the thought were a parting gift from Stella. But for Mia, life now was even more uneven in the middle than it had been at the beginning of it all. Certainly, this didn't bode well for the end.

What did she have to look forward to? She was sure, on this day, that whatever was out there waiting for her couldn't be good. Then again, maybe there wasn't anything, anymore, to look for. Maybe there wasn't anything else to understand. Time would pass. It always did. Yet now, as if it were a second heart, pumping out what would become her future, time seemed to have destroyed her past as surely as if it had never been at all. How, Mia wondered, do you untie the knots in your soul?

Mia had been right about one thing. All in all, the auction had been a disaster.

Part Two

February 2000

Although it's said to be bad luck to change the name of a horse, the string of names that follows a horse from owner to owner often reflects more the current owner's preference than any allusion to propriety or luck. Names change, but the horse remains the same.

Zack was happy with his new horse. It was the first Arabian he had ever owned and the only Arabian he had ever been around long enough to get to know, and after only a week he could tell the personality and ride were very different from his quarter horses.

But Zack was a cowboy kind of guy and he just couldn't ride a horse named Stella. She still had the faint star marking even though the chestnut coat had turned grey. Star was an obvious name, and after all, Jesse James and Butch Cassidy had both ridden horses named Star. Bat Masterson rode a horse named Stardust. And then there was the notorious Belle Starr. So, if he stretched it just a little, it could be a cowboy kind of name. So, Star it would be.

At three years old, Star had long ago lost her first foal chestnut coat and had gradually turned grey like her mother, dappled and darker at the points. Her unique star marking was gradually disappearing as her coat lightened, but the double swirls were still there.

Zack was interested in the change of color. It was also a matter of economics, since he intended to breed this new horse to his Palomino quarter horse stallion. And, his interest in genetics spoke volumes to his interest in veterinary medicine.

The genetics of grey are simple. In horses, melanin appears in two forms, eumelanin, or black, and phaeomelanin, or orange-red. These two pigments are the source of every horse color. Modifying genes cause them to be lighter or darker or to have white added in various ways. All horses have red pigment, although it can be modified or hidden, but only some horses have black pigment. Grey is not a color.

Grey horses start out as one of the base colors, with the grey gene added on top of the base color gene. Grey is actually a modifying effect. On the technical side, Zack knew it was at the "G" locus that there were two possible alleles, G and g. All non-grey horses are gg and all grey horses have at least one G. Since grey is dominant to non-grey, all grey horses must have at least one grey parent. Grey cannot skip generations and a horse with two grey parents may inherit a G allele from each, making it GG, or homozygous for grey. And if that happens, each of that horse's foals will be grey. This is where the questions came in concerning Star.

Zack had almost immediately lost her registration. He didn't really consider it lost yet, just misplaced somewhere really hard to find. It was not possible to tell exactly which alleles or allele combination created Star's grey coat just by looking, therefore finding her papers and lineage documentation was important to his ability to sell the foals for top dollar, foals he hoped would be Palomino. Palomino Arabian.

He knew that by about eight years Star would appear to be almost white, before the red specks, or fleabites, began to appear on her coat. But the dark skin under the coat, rather than the pinkish skin of a white horse, would always give her true color away. That dark skin would also protect her from the harsh Texas summer sun.

It's said there are two seasons in Texas, summer, and almost summer. Late April, known in Texas as almost summer, is spring at its best. And Zack was doing his best to extend the bright green days of early spring before the white-hot summer hammered down and ran humans and beasts alike in search of shade and breeze. It was days like this one though, that made Zack glad he lived in Texas.

He had spent a good deal of his spare time with his new horse. Because of their shortened backs and the mechanics of the way they moved their hind legs, Arabians aren't generally considered good roping horses, but Zack had read about a trainer in California who was training Arabians as cutting horses, and he liked what he had read. Both he and Star were game to give it a go.

For Star, western saddles were a different fit and feel from English tack. Heavy and cumbersome. A curb bit was not at all the same as a snaffle. It pulled in strange places on her mouth and chin, and the reins worked differently. But, she could adapt. If there was one thing Star did really well, on a human scale, it was her ability to change her attitude to adjust to circumstances and surroundings.

She knew it wasn't that she needed to change what was seen, what others saw, what glimmer might be observed, she just had to change the way she looked at it.

Once she accepted the rope whirling above her head, once she understood the concept of cutting, she was quick to forget the discipline of dressage. This was fun stuff.

Not that Zack had a clue as to how to work a dressage horse, he was all the same impressed with the way she moved and responded to the slightest pressure. Cutting took as much teamwork as dressage. It was about moving and thinking in tandem. It was about response time and the ability to think ahead. It was about interpreting the next move, it was about control. And Star was a horse in control.

Zack still lived on the ranch in east Hays County that had been in his family for four generations. His home was a single-wide trailer on the north edge of the property. He had tried to make it feel more like a home than what it was, and had built a redwood lattice awning that covered a wide front deck. Potted plants in brightly designed, hand-painted Mexican pots were placed by the entry. He had laid stones by hand around the deck to create a patio, and at the far end had dug a deep hole lined with brick for a fire pit.

When it wasn't too cold, and the stars were out, he liked to sit there, smoke a cigar, the burnt taste on his throat washed down with a cold bottle of beer.

A small creek defined one side of his acreage, and the ranch road that provided access defined the other boundary. He had carved a 35-acre, mostly rectangular tract out of the 400-acre ranch. And while he still had partial ownership rights to the rest of the ranch, it wasn't really home anymore. He had a 10 year-old blue heeler, a cat with one ear, 20 goats, and four horses including Star.

His brother James, who was 17 years older than Zack, lived in the family home with his wife, Lena, and their three children. It had been James who had taken care of Zack after their parents died. James was his big brother, but also a surrogate father and mother.

James oversaw the day- to-day operations of the ranch. It was his job to run the ranch and make sure it produced enough through hay and cattle sales to provide for him and his family and pay taxes on the land. It was his life, as it had been his parents', and embrace it or not, he knew that's the way it would always be unless he changed it. And he didn't see that happening.

James had been newly married when he took Zack in. Lena had been more than happy to have a child in the house. James hadn't seen it as a burden, but he did see it as a responsibility. He had also seen it, maybe used it as a reason, to stay where he was. At the time he had dreamed of leaving Texas with Lena and starting a new life, doing something fresh, his own creation, exciting, and almost anything other than ranching. It's not that he didn't love the ranch, but it was a hard life, and getting harder with every passing year. Then the babies started coming.

He loved them all, and he had always wanted a big intact family. That's exactly what he got. James knew life was capable of bringing pain all on its own. He saw it as his responsibility to respond by creating a life of joy. He was getting good at it.

Zack's parents had been gone long enough that there were some days he didn't consciously think about them. Then, something would be there, some essence, a whisper of the family that had been. It had been a good family, but other than his brother, Lena and their children, a few distant cousins, and an aunt and uncle he couldn't even remember, there wasn't much of it left.

This was Zack's life. He figured he had a long life to look forward to, but for some reason sensed, more often now than ever, that there wasn't much in it for him. At least not that he could see from where he was. He knew that what he felt, when he let himself feel at all, was at once a mix of what had been, who he was, and who he wanted to be. It was a memory, it was a fear, it was a nameless dread, and it was his introduction to the future. It was also a memory of some sort of happiness, for lack of a better definition, he had known at one time, and would for the rest of his life be in pursuit of. The past was always painting pictures in his head. Picasso had nothing on those pictures that ran through Zack's mind.

Animals were easy. They were easy to be around. They were kind, forgiving, unselfish and unpretentious. They were dependable. They didn't know how to hold a grudge. They carried no baggage. And horses were the best of all. They were his dreams, his desires, his own personal daily miracles. He thought he needed all the miracles he could get.

Whatever the secret was that everyone else seemed to know had escaped Zack. Not that he hadn't asked. He'd asked many times, in many ways. Sometimes silence, sometimes nothing, was the answer.

Maybe time trips us up. Maybe we're all exactly where we're supposed to be. And then again, maybe our human brains, for all of their brilliance and radiance, and all of their faults, aren't really designed to understand fully, what it is about now, what it is about today.

Zack was engaged to the Hays County Pork Chop Queen. They were the same age and had known each other forever. They had gone through school together, and the night they graduated from high school he had given her a tiny, little diamond ring. That's the way it worked, that's what Charlene had expected. Then.

Now, a little more than four years later, he wasn't sure why they were still engaged. He loved Charlene, but the relationship wasn't moving forward. It wasn't moving at all. Not that it was in a 'rut,' a word Charlene hated, and not that it wasn't 'comfortable,' a word she seemed to like a lot, it just never changed.

At the same time, Zack felt he had changed. He wasn't really sure how, but could just feel that he had somehow outgrown what had always been so 'comfortable.' He sort of wondered how much of his discontent was a result of the consequences of his own personal freedom. He was free, had been on his own a long time, and yet he was a prisoner of his own freedom. And was that, he wondered, the temptation of conflict or the essence of being human? Then again, perhaps it's all in how the issue is resolved that defines both.

Zack had attended day and night classes at Austin Community College and the University of Texas, and had applied to veterinary programs in Texas, Colorado and Louisiana. He enjoyed his job as a veterinary technician, but wanted and needed more of life. He wanted more for himself, he wanted to be able to do more, and he wanted to give more.

Charlene wanted more too. It's just that the "more" they wanted wasn't the same. They shared a history, but is history enough to sustain a lifetime together? Does an account of the past come close to the creation of a future?

Charlene had pointed out on more than one occasion that being the Pork Chop Queen was a lot of work. She always had to look good. She had to watch her weight. She was always "on." She had the pesky speaking engagements for the Pork Council trade shows. She had to put up with a lot of bad jokes. She had to be nice to everyone, except Zack, because after all, that was real life. And she had to be a role model for all the young girls who aspired to one day take her place.

One of Charlene's deepest secrets, one she hadn't even shared with Zack, was that she hated pork and hated pigs. They weren't cute. They were dirty, practically hairless and they smelled bad. All the time. The only reason she was Pork Chop Queen was because the thought of being Miss Armadillo was just too much. And, she had to be someone.

Charlene's other secret was that she wanted to go on to bigger things. She wanted to be Miss Hays County. She wanted to be Miss Texas. Most of all, she wanted to be Miss America. If only she could get Zack out of this cowboy thing. He needed a real job so he could support her efforts. Going to veterinary school in Charlene's mind was not a real job. It was school, and after that, it just meant more of the same, fooling around with a bunch of big, smelly animals.

Charlene won her first beauty pageant when she was four years old. She had three older brothers who had all made fun of her Miss Fourth of July costume. They had laughed louder and longer than anyone in the audience when her sparklers ignited her hair during her Yankee Doodle Dandy tap-dance routine. The hairspray had just been too much, the hair too big, and really, someone should have warned her mother that hairspray was flammable.

She'd been a trooper though. She still had the home movie of herself, stomping the offending sparkler to death, in time to the music yet, and then continuing her routine, sparkler-less, missing hardly a beat.

That had been her first title and her first introduction to fame, and it was all she'd needed to know that she was destined for bigger and better things. She was going to be somebody.

It had not been music or sparklers that had led her to win the Miss Hays County Pork Chop Queen title. But it had been patriotic.

Charlene had grown up and her sparklers had grown up as well. Twirling flaming batons to Lee Greenwood's "Proud To Be An American," tossing them high above her head, catching, spinning, jumping and landing in the splits, now that had kept the audience spellbound. The perky routine had been perfect, except for one thing. And it had all been Zack's fault.

"Go beautiful. Go girl. Spin that fire. Fire! Charlene! Fire!"

She would have been fine if she hadn't looked down. It hadn't been a real fire, just some smoldering and smoking lace crimlen. But she smacked it. She dropped the offending baton. OK, she sort of tossed it when she dropped it. OK, it sort of landed on the judges' table. It had just been a little fire.

Still, Charlene had her crown and Zack had spent the next few months making up.

But that was then. Water under the bridge. Let bygones be bygones. Yeah, right. Zack owed her.

Charlene loved Zack as much as she knew how to love anyone. And she knew Zack loved her, how could he not? Everyone loved Charlene. They always had. It was yet another thing she worked so hard at. Zack was lucky to have her. She had to make sure he didn't forget how lucky.

Of all her strategies, ploys and tactics, Charlene knew just which ones worked best with which people and which situations and knew exactly how to apply them for maximum effectiveness. Obviously, no one else knew what she was up to and she wasn't going to share. She considered her wiles part of her allure. And it wasn't as if she was a chronic or pathologic liar. She didn't consider her stories to be lies at all. They protected the innocent. It was all in the definitions. She could justify everything, and almost anything, because she knew her heart was in the right place.

Charlene lived by her own set of rules and personal standards, and she expected others to respect those rules. She couldn't cook, and didn't plan to start. She had no interest in cleaning. Gardening meant touching dirt and if she touched it long enough, it probably meant breaking a nail.

Animals were messy and usually had fleas or attracted flies. Horses were sweaty and tended to snort through their noses at her. Horses rolled in the mud, just like pigs. She didn't know what Zack saw in the big beasts.

It was in horses that Zack saw his future and his destiny. He loved horses, all horses. He had loved horses as a young child. He'd read Walter Farley, Richard Adams, Mary O'Hara, Sam Savitt, J. Frank Dobe and Marguerite Henry. He'd read Black Beauty five times and each time his eyes had filled with tears at every touching "horse moment." He'd ridden his stick horse all over the ranch, until his father had given him his first pony, Mr. Jones, on his fourth birthday.

No one was quite sure of Mr. Jones' age. Zack had kept and treasured him, cared for him and loved him, long after he'd quit riding him. When he was a junior in high school, he'd found him in the corral one evening, standing very still. At first he couldn't figure out what was wrong, why he wouldn't move, and then, he saw why.

Mr. Jones had somehow managed to break his shoulder. Not dislocate it, the grinding and movement of the bones indicated an almost crushing break. As best Zack could tell, the break involved the scapula at the shoulder joint and the top of the humerus.

Zack's grandmother had broken her hip when he was two, and had come to live with them briefly afterwards. He didn't remember much of it, but had learned later that it wasn't so much that the elderly tended to fall and break their hips, but that as people aged their bones became brittle and broke spontaneously, causing the fall.

Obviously, they hadn't put his grandmother down. But, she never really recovered either.

Zack had insisted that he be the one to put his beloved pony down.

It was the hardest thing he had ever done, before or since. Maybe it was because he had been the one to take Mr. Jones' life, even though it had to be done, maybe because he had the chance to say a final, wrenching, goodbye, but it had been more painful even than standing at his parents' graves, knowing they were gone from him forever. And, the sense of loss he felt when he thought of his parents, whisked with unfair finality from his life on a wet highway, was still so acute that at times it seemed he could not survive it.

Now, more often than not, what he felt was the culmination of all his losses, as if the essence of his life had cruelly been snatched away from him, leaving his heart, sore and raw.

What is there, in this world, that holds it, binds it all together? Zack knew there must be something to it. There had to be, or he'd managed to completely miss whatever point there was to be made. He was much too young to feel such a sense of hopelessness, but that's the way it was. That's the way he felt. And more than anything else he wanted it to change. His life was still too new, too young, to be weighted by the dryness that age brings, the dullness of too much time.

Zack had known very early on that caring for horses would somehow be a part of his life. In high school, he'd been active in FFA, and as a project had worked over a summer and then every afternoon thereafter throughout high school in a veterinary clinic. That had sealed it. As a large animal vet he could spend his time keeping horses healthy.

Zack too, had secret dreams. He wanted to specialize in treating performance horses.

And, now, today, in this place at this exact time, he knew he was standing on the edge of the rest of his life, not looking back, not quite sure where the future would take him or how it would take him there.

Zack held a letter in his hand from Colorado State University. He didn't want to open it. It wasn't the "skinny envelope" he'd received from Texas A&M, just like the one he received from LSU, but it wasn't as thick as he thought it should be if it contained good news.

Ever since Zack had been a little boy, he'd been drawn to horses when faced with a problem. It had started with Mr. Jones and there had been a steady progression of confidants throughout the years. Within just the last few weeks, it had become Star.

"What do you think, girl?" he asked.

It was feeding time, and the horses were milling in front of the feed room. Zack had Star off to the side, where he had stopped to talk with her. He was holding the envelope carefully since it seemed she wanted to taste it. Whatever was in there, he wanted it to stay intact until he'd worked up the courage to read it.

"If it crosses your path it's destined to be, and will leave something of itself behind forever, good or bad, right or wrong. Time and experience give us an advantage, rooted in not making the same mistake twice. And luck, luck carries the idea of randomness or maybe the whim of some tricky god who is toying with us. I don't like it, but it seems to be something of what people look for.

Zack knew he hadn't heard anything, no one had spoken, no one else was there. But, it seemed as if he actually heard the words that had just run through his mind. This had never happened before in all of his conversations with his horses. None of the horses had ever really answered. Zack had always carried both sides of the conversation, just to keep it going. It had been a game of pretend.

But this was a little different. The game of pretend had suddenly assumed its own set of rules.

"Better now than later," thought Zack. He held the envelope up, tried to look through it, thought if he prayed hard enough it would be enough to change the contents, if the contents needed changing.

"Prayer's not a vending machine. You don't just put your dollar in and out pops the miracle of choice. What's there is already there. It's up to you to do something with it."

This was getting weird. The voice wasn't male or female, and logically Zack knew it had to come from inside his own mind. But he could swear he heard it through his own two ears. Did he hear something real, something new, or was he hearing what he wanted to hear? Maybe it was more than he could listen to at one time, but there it was. And, there it seriously was.

Zack slipped his finger through the flap of the envelope, creating a jagged rip across the top. No paper cut. That was a good sign.

At first glance, it looked like it contained a two-page letter. He took it out, paused, said another quick prayer, and opened it. He closed his eyes before looking at the words, squeezed them shut, tightly, until the dark behind his eyelids turned to a bright light, then opened them. Focusing on the print, he saw only one word. "Congratulations."

Yes, thought Zack. Yes. It was a very good start. As he read the letter of acceptance he was aware of Star standing next to him, her whiskered chin almost touching his face, her breath warming his neck. It was as if she were trying to read the letter over his shoulder for herself.

"I'm in, girl. It says so right here. They want me. I'm going to be a vet."

Star nodded her head in either approval or impatience. Zack preferred to think of it as approval, but knew she was hungry and had already waited long, and patiently, enough. Besides, he wanted to get home and share the news with Charlene.

That's when he realized all the good news wasn't necessarily good.

This was his dream, and from what he had just read, it was going to be an expensive dream. No surprise there. It was going to take time and commitment. He knew Charlene loved him. He knew she wanted to get married. And he knew she had her own dreams. He knew Charlene was a high maintenance woman, and although she had never come right out and said so, he also knew she didn't think much of animals. It wasn't a happy thought to realize that she might not be nearly as enthusiastic with the news as he was.

Zack and Charlene didn't live together, but they may as well have. It seemed as if she was always at his place, or had been there, or would be there. She had her own apartment in San Marcos, but didn't spend much time in it. Actually, Zack thought it was a lot nicer than his trailer, but as far as he was concerned, not as comfortable. Charlene didn't like it when he moved things and didn't put them back. Her fashion magazines were perfectly lined up on the coffee table.

Six matching cushions were evenly spaced across the back of the sofa. A side chair sat at an exact right angle to the sofa. Obligatory knick-knacks from Pier One, Pottery Barn or World Market or some destination-sounding place were strategically placed on side tables and bookshelves. Silk flowers were arranged in a real vase of water, placed exactly in the center of the table in the dining area. That was what just killed him.

Zack had brought her a big bouquet of brilliant spring wildflowers once, thinking if she had real flowers she might not need the fake ones. He'd only done it once. She'd gingerly taken the flowers, holding them out from her as if they were stink weeds. "Bugs," was all she'd said, and she'd then set the flowers out on the back porch.

He pretended he didn't care, that his feelings weren't bruised, that her dismissal of his gift had nothing to do with him. But it had left a taste in his mouth he had not liked.

He never stayed over at Charlene's. She never asked. There wasn't much to eat except frozen dinners. When they were at his place, Zack cooked. He found it relaxing. After they ate, it was Zack who cleared away the dishes and cleaned up. Charlene never offered to help. Her nails were at stake.

He knew his brother and sister-in-law didn't care for Charlene. He knew they thought she was a poser, using him until someone better came along. And Zack knew there were plenty of "better" guys out there. But he really did care for her. She had been a part of him for so long, he didn't know how to think of himself without her. At the same time, he didn't know what she saw in him.

It wasn't that Zack thought so little of himself, but he would be the first to recognize and admit that he wasn't anyone special. He'd never done anything special. He'd never stood out. He mostly thought of himself as just someone else. Someone who had seen more unhappiness and felt more pain than seemed fair. He was. He existed. That was mostly it.

But now he was going to be someone he wanted to be. He was going to make something of the opportunity to be a veterinarian. He was finally going to get the chance to live a dream, his own dream, and he knew such chances happened seldom, if at all, in one's lifetime.

With the horses fed, Zack headed back to the house. He told himself if Charlene were there he'd take her out to eat to give her the good news. If she wasn't there, he'd fix dinner, get out the candles, and wait for her to show up, which he figured would be around 7pm. He even had a bottle of red wine, and Charlene liked wine a lot better than beer, especially with pasta, which was one of the six things Zack knew how to make. She seemed to never run out of opportunities to explain to Zach the differences between her tastes and preferences and his, and what this stood for, and why it was important. Zach didn't really understand, but for all involved, pretended to appreciate the importance of the distinction.

Charlene wasn't there.

Zack was almost relieved.

He set about to fix dinner. Rigatoni pasta with marinara sauce. He minced fresh tomatoes, onions, garlic, basil and peppers out of the garden Lena and the kids kept. He added water and olive oil for the broth. Then a little red wine he kept in the refrigerator just for sauces. Turning the burner to simmer, he filled the pasta pot with water and a little salt and olive oil.

Next, he took a loaf of French bread out of the freezer, cut it in half, and put half back in. He sliced the remaining half in rounds, buttered them, and coated the top with the rest of the minced garlic and a little parmesan cheese. That too, was set aside, to go in the oven at the last minute after the pasta cooked.

Zack set the table for two, using matching dishes, wine glasses and forks. He had started out with four of everything, a gift from Lena, but as one or another had broken or been chewed up by the disposal, and had then been replaced with something only closely resembling the original, finding a matched set wasn't easy. At least the candles matched.

He was ready.

An hour later, Zack was sitting in his lawn chair, two empty long necks at his feet and another about to join the crowd. He was watching the sunset eat up the atmosphere, waiting for Charlene. She was always there for dinner. He knew she'd show eventually. And he knew she'd be hungry, even though she would feign indifference.

The dust kicked up further down the road, and Zack knew Charlene was on the way. He'd decided to wait until they were well into dinner to break the news.

Small talk of the day, who said what, who did what took ten minutes. The description of a new pair of boots and a sweater with leather trim at the cuffs and neckline, already safely packed away for fall in Charlene's closet, took five more minutes. The real and pressing need to find a tweedy fall skirt to go with it, and the importance of the overall look, another five minutes. A co-worker's pending marriage plans accounted for another five.

Finally, in the silence that resulted from Charlene's break to chew and swallow, it was Zack's turn.

"I have news," said Zack. "Good news."

"Well for goodness sake, what is it?"

Zack pulled the letter out of his pocket and held it up. "I'm in. Colorado State at Fort Collins accepted my application. I'm going to veterinary school, Charlene."

Charlene could have been eating lemons given the look on her face. Zack knew immediately she was going to have plenty to say. Where was the blind eye, the deaf ear, when you needed it?

"You can't go to school, Zack. It's too far and it will take too long. Why can't you just get a nice job in Austin like everybody else? Why do you want to be a veterinarian anyway? They're just animals. It's not like you were going to be a real doctor."

Should he tell her? Should he tell her about Star? About what he thought she told him? What could he lose now?

"Charlene, this may sound crazy, but it's my calling. It's what I'm supposed to do. You won't believe this but I was out with the horses when I got this letter, and I swear, Star said as clear as day, "If it crosses your path, it's destined to be. Go for it."

Charlene just stared at him, her mouth slightly open, her eyes almost wild.

"Charlene, come on honey. Forget what Star said. Forget I said anything. Just my imagination anyway. You know this is what I've dreamed about. You know me better than anyone. Come with me. Fort Collins is a big city. You'll find a job there. We can get married."

The words just kept coming.

"Zack, we can't get married with you in school. You'll be too busy studying all the time. You probably won't have time for a job, and then it will all be on me and I'll work too hard and start looking old and worn out and won't win any titles anymore. I'll never get to be Miss America."

Zack almost felt sorry for Charlene. Now she was sniffling. In a few minutes her eyes would fill with tears. He knew it was easy for Charlene to cry when it suited her. It was a talent she'd perfected in second grade and it was a maneuver he'd found attractive, about ten years ago.

"Charlene, you don't have to be Miss America. How about Mrs. Holder instead?

"No," said Charlene. "No, it won't work. I don't want to go to Colorado and I don't want you to go either."

It seemed to Zack that the bridge of language he'd tried to build to cross all the objections and incongruities he thought he might encounter was not nearly as strong as he had hoped.

"You owe me, Zack. You can't do this," said Charlene, more quietly than before. "I've given up so much for you. You can't just go off now and leave me."

"I don't want to leave you, Charlene. I want you to come with me. And, besides, you haven't given anything up for me. You always do just what you want to do."

He knew as soon as he said it that the choice of those exact words would be interpreted as a challenge. Now the discussion was over, and the real argument would begin.

And Charlene instinctively knew it was time for the big guns.

"Not true," said Charlene. "Remember when I had the flu our senior year? How it kept coming back? I was sick on and off for almost three weeks. Well, it wasn't the flu."

"What are you talking about? That was four, almost five years ago. Why'd you say it was the flu? What was it? What does that have to do with going to veterinary school?"

"Don't be such a dolt. What do you think it was? It was a baby. A baby, Zack. And I got rid of it. For you. So you wouldn't be tied down."

And that was it. The silence sat there between them like an unwelcome guest Zack wished would go home. Zack stared at Charlene, and she defiantly stared back.

"You made that up. I hope you just made that up," said Zack. It sounded stupid but it was all he could think of. "You would have told me."

"I almost did. I tried, but then I couldn't. I knew you'd want to get married right away, and it just wasn't right. We hadn't even graduated yet. There was so much I still wanted to do. Remember, I was trying for that modeling contract? And you, all you talked about was going to college and being a vet. We couldn't have a baby. We were still kids. I just couldn't. I couldn't throw my life away that quickly."

"We were the same age as my parents when James was born," said Zack. "We could have made it work. You should have told me, Charlene. Whatever decision we would have made, I had a right to know." Dinner conversation was no longer quiet, or especially civilized.

Zack pushed his chair back and stood up, picked up his half-finished plate and carried it to the sink. He didn't turn around, couldn't turn around. He didn't want Charlene to see his tears.

He'd had no choice in it, nothing to say. He'd lost a child, a son or daughter, and never even known it. Of all his losses in life, now he was losing that which he'd never had. And now, all of a sudden, he was supposed to make sense of something he didn't understand.

Where was sincerity when you needed it? Were his feelings about what he had just heard, from a person he thought he loved, to be doubted? And did that mean he had to doubt his own honesty, his own integrity? He didn't think so, but was he such a fool that he had never had a clue? And if he was to be a part of what had happened, even happening now, for him, for the first time, he somehow knew he couldn't, wouldn't betray himself. The deception was too much to take in all at once.

"Well, I guess now you know why you can't leave," said Charlene.

How could this seem so simple for her? How could she talk about it as easily as if she'd said it was getting ready to rain? Had it been so easy when she'd made her decision four years ago, a decision he'd had no say in at all?

He should have known, should at least have suspected. He saw himself as much a part of it as Charlene, even though he had known none of it at the time. His unborn child may have been baptized by tears, years later it seemed, but it was Zack and Charlene who were washed with blame.

Zack had never really thought about abortion in terms of absolutes, right or wrong. He believed people had the right to do what they felt was right for everyone involved. But that definition meant being involved in making the decision. He had been left out.

A cotton haze seemed to fill his head and mouth. It hurt to breathe. The trailer had never been so small, and it was closing in on him fast.

Zach was contemplating one of those puzzling questions that mankind has agonized over for eternity. Some people care and others are not bothered by theological or spiritual challenges. Most human brains aren't designed to at once take it all in, reserving the mysteries for future explanation. Maybe the problem was with time.

Taking time out of the equation made sense. If all events happened in present time, he could change the outcome. But, the outcome of this event wasn't subject to time. It had happened. It was history, it was eternal. It was where time falls away.

"Charlene, I think you better leave, and leave now. I don't know what I'm going to do next, and you don't want to be here to find out. Go on. Leave. Just leave me the hell alone."

"Zack."

"No. Just go."

"Zack?"

"Get out. Now."

The door slammed harder than Zack thought the frame would stand. The thin walls of the trailer shuddered. Charlene's Mazda spit gravel as it sped down the drive.

Speed had a sound of its own. Zack pictured his parents, hit head-on by a drunk kid in a pickup, going too fast, trying to get away from, or headed toward, what? So long ago, and it seemed as if the past kept teasing him with the present. It just wouldn't let go.

Zack didn't understand how his life could be so suddenly changed. Once again. With just a few words, everything was different. He didn't know if he could forgive Charlene, whether it was his place to do so, and he wasn't even sure if there was anything anymore to forgive. He didn't know what to think, how to feel, how he should feel. He wasn't sure just what he felt at the moment for Charlene, or if he felt anything at all other than hurt and betrayal. She had been so much of him for so long, it was as if he were no longer the person he had been just half an hour before. Over something decided and finished almost five years ago, announced over a plate of pasta.

Zack found himself thinking about Sunday School.

He'd gone to Sunday School every Sunday when he was seven, because he was too fidgety to sit through an entire church service. He'd liked the coloring and pasting part and he'd mostly liked sitting in the circle listening to the stories that made up the lesson. But out of that entire year, only one story had stuck with him, and he still remembered it.

It was the parable comparing the life of Jesus to a department store, where someone sneaks in during the night and changes all the prices around. In the morning, the things of great value suddenly have ridiculously low prices. The items of little value are now those with incredibly high prices.

For some reason that was never really explained, no one notices the change. Life goes on. Before long, everyone's lived with the mixed up prices for so long that they just accept the prices as true. Not only were they accepted, they were believed. And every day, all the people with their busy, hectic and often self-centered lives, just revolve around and around the values contained in those mixed up prices.

There had been a moral to the story, but Zack had been more fascinated with the idea that no one had noticed, or questioned the change, in the first place.

That had been Zack's life, up to now. And now what? How much more mixed up could things get?

Zack scraped the food on the dishes into the garbage and piled them in the sink. He took the bottle of wine and headed to the barn. If horses were to be his life, then that's where he would start putting it back together.

It was dark in the barn, and he didn't want to turn on the light. There was comfort in the dark. He liked the horse noises as they shuffled and shifted and snuffed in the night. Paxton, his Palomino stallion was finishing his hay. He was a serious eater, and acknowledged Zack's presence with a snort, but didn't leave his feeder.

Both mares were pregnant, and they too munched with great gusto. Then there was Star.

She turned toward the sound of his footsteps and let out a soft nicker. As Zack approached, she lifted her head and blew softly at his face. She seemed to have lost interest in the hay, seemed to give Zack her attention, seemed to sense that he needed it.

"Hey girl. Hey there. Well, here's a real mess. I knew she might not be real happy about me going to school, but this, man, this is something else. I never would have thought something like this was possible. I don't know what to do. What can I do? Now that I know the truth, I wish I didn't. I wish she'd never told me, but then I'd be living the lie with her. I just wouldn't know it.

"So, now what? What's next? What do I do?"

Zack took a good slug of wine. He didn't expect an answer. But it felt good to pose the questions out loud, to get them out of his head where they were pounding.

"If you knew what I know you'd understand how even the simplest truth isn't simple. You'd see how any truth could well be a lie. You don't really want to know, not the big truth, not the real truth. It's not something you, or anyone else can live with. It just is."

Zack didn't believe for a minute that Star had answered him. He knew it was his own voice in his own mind. But the words were not his words. It was back to his old game of pretend. He was getting better at it.

Zack related the events of the evening. It somehow made it easier to accept to say it all out loud, made it more real, turning it into something he thought he might be able to make some sense of.

"Like it or not, you can only live by moving forward, you understand by looking back. The thing is, you need to do both, in balance, with hope and grace. Just don't lose sight of either."

Zack drank more wine. The bottle was close to empty. He was sure it was the wine talking in his head, but even so, he still didn't know what to think, do, or how to move forward.

"Time, hope, opportunity, the future, comes like a thief, the heavens will pass away with a roar, and the heavenly bodies will be burned up and dissolved, and the earth and the works that are done on it will be out."

Now it was scripture. If this was it, all of it and out in the open, it was done. It was out of his hands. Whose hands it was in exactly, was a new question.

Zach was becoming more and more convinced as the night went on, that he and Charlene weren't going to have a fairy tale ending. Most fairy tales have happy endings, endings that play to the basic instincts and needs of hope and faith, of good triumphing over evil, of happily ever after. He and Charlene would just end, each experiencing their own ending, and each starting a new beginning.

And, he didn't think it would end anywhere near happily ever after.

Zack remembered reading the story of Thomas Edison and all the false tries he made when inventing the light bulb. When asked why he kept trying after so many failures, Edison's answer revealed that he saw things from a different perspective. He didn't see the failed attempts as mistakes, but rather as the elimination of wrong solutions. Maybe that was Zack and Charlene.

For Zack it seemed that making mistakes, and he had made his share, held a wealth of knowledge, and once he figured out what to do with it, he knew it would be a valuable lesson learned. Maybe he had overlooked all the closed doors or circumstantial signs that now were so obvious. Had he stood on foolishness instead of faith? And how would he ever know what the ultimate outcome was to be? How would he really know when over was ultimately over?

But, these were questions for the future. For now, Zack felt he was finally just beginning to get it right. It was his time.

Things didn't look any brighter in the morning.

Zack had a hangover from too many beers and most of the bottle of wine. He'd gone to bed late, and after dozing off finally around 4 am, was awake again at 5:30.

He was good at saving tomorrow for tomorrow, but what about today?

It was early May. He had until September to figure out how to move to Fort Collins, and how to pay for school. He knew he could get a student loan to cover most if not all of the tuition. He could find a cheap apartment. He could get a job. But he wanted to do this right. He wanted to have plenty of time to study. He needed money in the bank, more than he had in his checking account, which barely got him through each month.

Zack planned to sell the goats. Most of the females were pregnant, so he would get a good price for the herd. He had the two mares that would foal within the next few weeks. He hoped James would take Paxton. And there was Star. She was valuable. He'd paid $2,500 for her and that had been a bargain. He should be able to get at least that much back.

Selling Star wasn't something Zack wanted to do, but his brother had balked at taking on one horse. Two were out of the question.

That was it. That was about all Zack had. He needed his truck for transportation. Couldn't sell that. He'd pack his bed, TV and few belongings in the horse trailer, and the single-wide wasn't even his. Not much to show for 23 years, but that would change.

And then there was Charlene. What was he going to do about Charlene?

He knew she would be icy cold and breathing fire over being kicked out last night. She wouldn't see that any of it had been her fault. With Charlene, nothing ever was. You either adored that about her, or you accepted it for what it was. He had started off adoring it, but had to admit that lately, more often than not, it had become harder to take. There just wasn't any way to negotiate affection.

There was no doubt in Zack's mind that he was going to Fort Collins. There was also no doubt that he would be going alone. And that pretty much answered the Charlene question. Letting her in on the answer was something else.

Charlene too, had been thinking. She was trying to decide what to do about Zack. There was no way she was going to Fort Collins, and no way she was going to hang around and wait while he went to school. She knew in her heart of hearts that he would miss her, and as soon as he was all alone, he would want her back, want her company once again. But she knew too, that by then, she would have moved on as well. Charlene wasn't one to ever make a move backwards and once a decision was made, it was final.

But telling Zack when he wouldn't talk to her, telling him something he didn't want to hear, that would take some doing. And it would take doing quickly.

Charlene didn't like to leave things hanging. No loose ends. All sorts of opportunities might be right around the corner, getting ready to bang on her door, and she wanted to be ready.

After three days, Zack figured it was time. Charlene had either cooled down, or not, but he had to do what he had to do, and what he had to do was bring things to some sort of conclusion.

Charlene was cool. Zack had known she would still be angry, but he could sense more than that in her voice. Still, she must have wanted to talk to him since she answered the phone on the second ring, and with Caller ID, she hadn't had to answer at all.

"We need to talk this through. I don't want to leave it hanging out there any longer. You want to meet me somewhere? You want me to come there?"

"Zack." It was a statement. "Let's meet at City Café. It's not too loud. We can talk. Be there at 6:00 and we can beat the dinner crowd." Another statement, this one bordering on an order.

Zack wanted to be there first. He wanted to see her when she walked in, to get a fix on her mood and attitude. He arrived at 5:45, got a table and ordered a beer. Charlene was late. By 6:15 he wondered if she had changed her mind, but at 6:20 the waves parted and Charlene headed to the table. She looked determined, but not especially friendly or happy, certainly not happy to see him.

Zack ordered another beer and a glass of Chardonnay for Charlene. It was a new and awkward situation. Charlene jumped in. Zack had known she would, and for this, he was grateful.

"Well, this is new."

"How so?"

"Us. How we are. What we both have to say and don't want to say. So, I'll just say it. You're disappointed. You're leaving. I'm disappointed. I'm staying. I guess this means we're over. Maybe we've been over and just didn't know it. Maybe this is for the best. Whatever, I guess it's the way it is."

From somewhere inside, Zack knew these were words he wanted to hear, but they were also words full of a new sadness. He looked at Charlene and for the first time thought of how small her sense of self, of usefulness, really was. He was moved, but it was more by the sense of parting than by the recognition that they were through.

"You're right, Charlene. Maybe this is why we never got married. Maybe we knew this, or something like it, was coming. I wish you the best, I really do, and I know you'll have it. You never settle for anything less. I know someday I'll open the paper, and there it will be, right on the front page, you in your Miss America crown."

He'd finally said just the right thing.

July, 2001

It was done, all of it. The mares and foals, other than Star, were sold. The goats were sold. Paxton was settled in at his brother's place. He was almost packed. Before he loaded the trailer he would drop Star off at the clinic where she would stay until he could sell her. Zack had five days before he was to leave. He still didn't have papers for her, and had given up on finding them. He would get what he could. Without the papers he knew it wouldn't even be a thousand dollars.

Zack knew he would miss his horses, and in a way he would miss the life he had lived for so long. It all worried him, the unknown. But what he was moving toward was a better life. It was a life of dreams. He knew it would be what he hoped it to be. He just had to make it happen.

It was time to load Star, and she didn't want to get in the trailer. She was going to make it harder on him than it already was. He tugged, he filled the hay net with hay, he pushed, he offered an apple. She didn't budge.

"Come on, you. Get in there. What's the matter with you today?"

"Today is a special place. A vulnerable place. It's your place, my place, our place. Yesterday and tomorrow are no different."

And with that, she calmly walked into the trailer.

Zack settled her into the stall and run-out at the clinic that would be her home until he could find a buyer. He had placed flyers at the local feed stores and on the bulletin board at the post office. Someone had already called and would be there in the morning to look at her. He felt better knowing that the veterinarians and staff at the clinic would take care of her until she was sold. Maybe tomorrow would be the day. There was no room in his life here for sentiment, yet it was sentiment that drove him. It was sentiment he had to overcome, and at the same time, sentiment he had to heed.

And so it was. Two women, one with a little girl, showed up to look Star over. It was obvious the woman with the daughter was the potential purchaser. It was also very clear that she had never owned a horse before, and intended, full steam ahead, to own one now. The other woman already owned and bred Arabians and seemed to know the breed. Star would board at her place until her new quarters were ready.

Questions were asked, some had answers. An offer was made and accepted and Star was sold.

Zack loaded her in his trailer to take her to her new, temporary home. Her new owner still had to renovate a barn and put up a corral fence to make the improvements needed for horses.

To Zack, Star seemed alert and impressed with the herd of Arabians she would be living with for the next few months. Whinnies were exchanged and Star fairly danced into her private run-out stall.

Zack's eyes were moist. He had never kissed a horse, and he wasn't going to start now. But Star was a special horse. They shared a special bond, they had shared more than that, but he didn't know what to think of it, how to describe it. Instead, he gently massaged the tips of her ears, whispered goodbye, and rested a hand, tenderly and for just a moment, on her face.

"It's OK. No one is lucky enough to live long enough to see the results of all that he has done. You'll never get that guarantee. Still, without taking the chance, without risking the worst, what will you find out?"

Zack just shook his head.

And that was that. It was time to find out. It was time to start a new life.

Part Three

Narrator

August 2001

Milagro De la Estrella De Dominga. Sunday Star Miracle. Estrella. Stella. Star. Star had a new owner, and once again, a new name—Star-Baby, soon to be The Lovely and Talented Star-Baby.

And I had my first horse. Finally. It only took 43 years.

I don't know exactly how it came about that I'm involved in this part of the story, how I became a piece of it or what I have to offer. Fate perhaps, chance, purpose, simple coincidence, horse sense, or luck? Surely there are many other far more deserving people out there who would have been a more appropriate choice, capable of doing a better, more eloquent job, people who could recognize and understand what they were up against.

Then again, maybe reasons why aren't as central to understanding as recognizing the questions in the first place. I'm never short of questions.

But, nonetheless, here it is.

Horses have always been a big part of my life. Every Christmas I would pray, yes, really pray, for months in advance, hoping with the most fervent expectations to find a horse in the living room, or at least tied to a tree in the backyard. Instead, there were stuffed horses, ceramic horses, horse books, paint by number horses and horse models that snapped together and could then be glued, sniffed and painted. But the closest my parents, or Santa, ever came was the Christmas there was a Clippity Clop Wonder Horse on giant springs with large wooden pegs sticking out of the side of its head, sitting under the tree by my pile of Santa loot.

I was six, and mounted Clippity Clop with the fluid skill of an Indian brave. My sister, always wanting what I had, wanting to do what I did, decided immediately that it was her turn. She grabbed the springs to stop my hell bent ride. It didn't take long for my parents to see the error of their ways as they iced my sister's red, pinched fingers. My mother, in all her wisdom, couldn't resist pointing out once again, that horses were just too dangerous.

When I wasn't trying to talk my parents into buying a horse, I would pester my dad to take me riding. That worked about once a month. I'm surprised it worked that often since the closest and most available stables were on the levee in uptown New Orleans. As soon as we hit the top of the levee, I was off at full gallop. It was a yee-haw, cowgirl kind of thing. He would spend the rest of our allotted hour calling me back, to slow down, to wait for him. I always pretended I couldn't hear him, that it was the horse that kept running off. I don't think he bought a bit of it, but still we kept going back.

My father was really my horse ally. It was a strong father-daughter bond. As an officer candidate in basic training after the start of World War II he'd ridden a big, black horse named Dr. Pepper. The ever-expanding, bigger and ever-more-dangerous exploits and adventures of Dr. Pepper were my bedtime stories. They wove themselves into my dreams, my desires, my wishes, my very existence. I really thought if I worked hard enough I could wear him down, that one day, instead of a new bicycle, he'd take me out and we'd buy a horse. We had a two-car garage and a backyard. What more did we need?

When I was ten, we entered a contest to win a distant but still genuine offspring of Native Dancer. All you had to do was send in an entry form with a name for the foal, along with a Corona cigar band. How hard could that be? My father did more than his share to support the cigar industry and bought those cigars by the box. Such sacrifice on his part. And, I was so sure we would win that foal, I'd already made a pallet on the floor by my bed where the foal would sleep. I was still young enough and naive enough to believe that if you wanted something that badly, prayed hard enough, and didn't hit your brother or sister, good things would happen for you.

Having to face reality, the reality of letting go of those dreams, is one of the hardest and cruelest things life does to you. It follows you forever, reminding you of its presence, reminding you that not everything you try to achieve will be within your reach. How hard you try, how much you plan or plead or beg, how good you promise to be isn't even a factor.

Lessons in life are hard and one of the hardest is to finally realize that life isn't perfect, no matter how fervently we try to make it so. It's actually a pretty messy place to be, and despite our best intentions, it's incapable of perfection. We wear ourselves out striving for that perfection, which seems more to come about from a well-hidden sense of inadequacy.

And that's where gratitude comes in. When we begin to feel a sense of gratitude, and accept life for what it is, with all its imperfections, the world becomes right. We are able to seize the joy of the world and our place in it. But, I still really wanted that horse.

I graduated from high school. No horse. I graduated from college. No horse. Masters degree. No horse. Marriage. Still no horse. And no luck talking my beloved husband into it either. The man I married wasn't a horse person. Yet.

A move from one state to another. Twin daughters. Another move, and then yet another. This time to the Texas Hill Country, to a place with a barn. Suddenly, real possibilities loomed.

And, finally, almost miraculously, a horse. My very own horse.

Our hill country veterinarian's assistant had been admitted to veterinary school in Colorado and was selling his horse for tuition. A friend with Arabians called to tell me about the horse. She was going over to look at her and wondered if I was interested?

Was I interested? Was August in Texas hot? Was I still breathing?

And, this horse was affordable. The owner had lost her papers. Who needed stupid papers? He'd bought her at auction, and the auction house only kept duplicates for six months. The original owners were out of business and couldn't be located. He was open to an offer.

I made an offer.

From the first time I saw her it was as if she were all at the same time a link to my past, to my childhood dreams and to my dreams still, and to my future. I looked into her gold-flecked, gentle black-brown eyes and saw the universe. They were soft, soulful, innocent eyes, yet at the same time held a whisper of everything that existed, had ever existed or ever would exist in the world. Maybe I was just in love with her. Maybe I would have been as much in love with any horse, but I don't think so. This was my horse, and she was special. I knew it from the start.

I don't know what she saw in me other than a pushover with a never ending supply of carrots, apples and chewy, gummy, candy orange slices, but in her I suddenly, unexpectedly saw today as a place in time that touches eternity. We had crossed paths, she had broken into my soul, it was destined to be, and whatever else it was, I knew already that it would leave something vital and essential of itself behind forever.

My offer was accepted. Her owner, Zack, loaded my new horse into his trailer and hauled her to my friend's barn, where she would stay until we could get ours' ready for a horse.

One of my daughters, the horse-lover, had-to-have-a-horse daughter, had gone with me to look at "the horse." Now, she considered it to be her horse too.

I'm not a selfish person, but I wasn't about to share my new horse with anyone, not even my own daughter. Some things are just too special to share.

We teach our children to share their toys. We tell them that it builds character, makes them better people, and actually increases the amount of fun they can have, because they have someone to share it with. I felt bad about not sharing my new horse, so bad, I didn't quite have the nerve to shatter her horse-dream without a ready solution. I had an idea.

It was brilliant if I do say so. No one else knew it yet, but our herd would grow in just a few weeks. I wasn't sure how, but that was the plan.

We settled Star into her new temporary quarters. I didn't want to leave, but kissed her goodbye, hugged her neck, probably too hard, and headed off to buy a halter and lead and call my husband at work to tell him the good news.

"Guess what? We're horse people!"

Silence on the other end. Then, "what do you mean exactly by, we're horse people?"

I had a great life. I've always considered it to be special. The most ordinary things became exceptional, the usual became unusual, the mundane, brilliant. My husband and I are still on our honeymoon, although at the time I acquired our first horse we'd been married for 21 years. Our eleven year-old daughters were nearly teenagers. They knew more than their parents, more than their teachers, and they didn't understand why everyone around them couldn't see what they knew to be true. But they had big hearts and their hearts were in the right places.

So what was missing?

Why did I need or want that horse so badly? Because I did. I always had. I just had to have a horse. If you're not a horse person, you won't understand. It's more than having to have a Mercedes, or a Porsche, or a tennis bracelet from Tiffany's. It's more than having to have a home entertainment center with risers, a 70-inch LED HDTV and surround sound. It's more than vacationing at the latest 'to be seen in' spot. If you are a horse person, you know exactly what I mean. There's something extraordinary about a horse. Your own horse.

And you know too, how frustrating it can be when your dream isn't exactly as you always pictured it.

I took guitar lessons from the age of 8 to 14, because I wanted to be a cowboy (not cowgirl, although technically that's all I could be, but, cowboy), mostly because everyone knows cowboys ride horses all day, what better life could there be, and cowboys play the guitar at night by the campfire, leaning back against their saddles, their faces warmed by the glow of the fire. I could just picture my trusty horse, standing there behind me, head hanging down, listening, at the ready for anything and everything. Ha.

Not my new horse. Not the perfect horse of my dreams.

First she stepped on my foot. It was the kind of pain that comes with shooting stars, nausea and a fear of looking down to see if part of your foot was missing. I was flexible. I marked that down to my fault for putting my foot in the wrong place. Still, with three broken toes and two black soon to be missing toenails, it was a rocky start.

I bought a fine old used roping saddle, new saddle pad, headstall and friendly D-ring snaffle bit. I bought a hoof pick and brushes, a turquoise halter and multi-colored cotton lead rope. I bought apple wafer treats and stocked our refrigerator with four varieties of apples, so I could determine which she most preferred, and plenty of carrots. I spent hours ruining my nails saddle soaping and oiling that saddle to soften it up so it wouldn't be too stiff for her tender back.

First ride, she threw me. That was after she bit me, hard, while I was cleaning her hooves with my brand new hoof pick. The target speaks for itself. I told myself I was doing something wrong. Must be the wrong kind of bit, maybe the saddle was too heavy, maybe she was used to different reining or leg control patterns. Maybe my hands were too hard for her tender, young mouth. Maybe she was trying to tell me something and I didn't know what to listen for, or how to hear.

I talked to all the horse people I knew, and they all had advice, and of course, none of it was the same.

"Beat the hell out of her. Show her who's boss." I didn't think so.

"Use a curb bit and chain. That'll give you better control."

"Here's an extra tie-down you can borrow. She can't throw you if she can't throw her head up."

"She's getting too much grain. She's too hot. Switch to racehorse oats."

While it may have all been good advice, it didn't seem to be the right advice. It didn't feel right. I didn't try any of it. But who was I to say? My experiences ended with stable horses and Clippity Clop, the Wonder Horse.

I decided to do it my way. I needed to get to know this horse. At the same time, I had the sneaking suspicion that I may have gotten in just a little over my head with "too much horse." I didn't say that, and I would never admit it. I had what I had always wanted. Little did I know what I'd really gotten in to. But, I already loved her. We were stuck with each other, and I wasn't about to begin to admit to anyone, including myself, that I'd made a mistake. Besides, I've always liked a challenge.

So we walked. We took long walks every day, it was much like walking a dog, a really big dog who likes to tug. While we walked I talked, and watched, and listened. I noticed things like sticks on the ground that set her off. Pieces of plastic bags on branches set her off. Windy days set her off. Culverts were a problem. She didn't like puddles. She didn't like snakes. She didn't like bicycles. She really hated goats.

"It's all right, Star-Baby. It's OK." The words themselves became almost a mantra.

Star-Baby she became.

And along the way, she grew more calm, more trusting, and I, more confident. We were communicating on some raw, undefined, fundamental level. Who knew?

Things were different. We were riding again, and we were together. We had a lot of respect for, and maybe a little healthy fear of each other, but whatever it was, it worked. I got to decide where we went. Star-Baby mostly behaved. We both kept an eye out for long sticks, pieces of plastic, puddles, culverts and goats, but before long, even those demons weren't so scary.

I loved this horse, and I had convinced myself she loved me right back. After each ride, or grooming, she would rub her head, hard, up and down my shoulders, arms and back. I know it was because her head itched and she considered me to be her personal tree, but I liked it. I liked the attention. I liked the interaction.

Everyone else told me to slap her off, that she was getting too familiar. Somehow, that just didn't seem nice. So we continued on, doing things "our" way, and our relationship continued to develop. I hadn't known any horses the way I knew Star-Baby, so I didn't know to what levels horse-human relationships could rise, but I had the feeling ours would continue to grow deeper, more profound and stronger still over time. Could I have been more green, or any more naïve?

Finally, the barn was ready, and it was time to bring her home. We brought her new stable mate, our new, new horse, Bullet, home on the same day.

It was a nothing kind of ad in our local weekly three-page paper that got our attention. We didn't subscribe to the paper because there was never anything in it but local ads, but the publisher was sending it out free for a month to boost subscriptions. I don't even know why I opened it that day, or bothered to glance at the ads, but I did. And there it was, "Palomino quarter horse gelding. Gentle. Great for kids or beginners. Must sell." Our typical response, "Well it doesn't hurt just to go look."

He was standing in a muddy little makeshift enclosure with an electric hot wire run loosely around the perimeter, stapled to whichever trees were most convenient to create a pen. A wet, brown and moldy, cattle grade round hay bale was plopped in the center. There was no shelter. Two other ribby horses shared the pen.

His name at the time was Bullet, and he didn't at all look the part. He just stood there. But there was a gleam in his eyes, a glimmer of who he had been, or could be again. He might be down, but he wasn't quite out.

We had to take him. We had to put meat back on those bones. We had to give him a good home. Just look at him. You could tell he deserved it.

The herd was growing. Two horses. Although only Star-Baby was technically mine, I knew I now had two horses. Life was good.

Bullet, or Bubba, as he quickly came to be called, was a gentleman, a real pill, yet at the same time, a ladies' man. An ex-ranch horse, he'd spent about a month at a children's riding camp. It had been one month too much. There was a lot we didn't know about him, but we did know Bubba wasn't a 'kick you in the sides and yell giddy-up' kind of horse. He was a 'toss you in the air if you tried that sort of thing' horse. Not suitable for little ruffians. Very suitable for husband and daughter. They had a healthy fear of and respect for horses. They knew better.

The day the horses came home was the coldest day of the season. The highs were only in the mid-20's. This was maybe a normal January in some parts of the country, but not in central Texas, where a high of 60 degrees was more normal than not. The wind was relentless and the wind chill had to be at least 10 below zero. It was that cold. Dust and caliche flew in little make-believe clouds, stinging, choking and eye-watering.

By the time the horses had decided, in their own horse-fashion who got which stall, and had kicked a hole smack-dab in the front of the brand-new siding in the process, it was almost dark. Feeding reassured them both that they were in a good place. The sunset flamed at the bottom of the sky. The day was gone. Darkness had arrived. But with the dark came the light. Of sorts.

Star-Baby had never seen stars, she had never been out under the stars at night. She had always been stabled, with the exception of the ill-fated auction when her mother had been killed. It had stormed both nights during the auction in Amarillo, and the sky had been black. So a sky lit by stars was new to her. Her new stall was an open box stall where she was free to leave its cover and protection and roam around the corral. The stars overhead blanketed the sky like a snow-globe that had just been shaken up, without interference from city lights.

With great interest and curiosity she watched the flickering stars come out against the dark backdrop of the universe, and waited for what would happen next. As the evening winds died down with the night, a gentle breeze seemed to set the inert universe in motion, creating patterns and illusions from the light generated by the stars.

Then there were voices. So many voices all at once, so much for her to take in. All the teachers, all the knowledge, and each way to interpret the applications, brought to her in a universe filled with a chorus of awareness, consciousness and understanding. The stars began speaking with each other, speaking of truths and realities and ideals and values. It was all very strange, new, and very wonderful. Star-baby listened.

"Truth," whispered the closest star, not really all that close, "is to act in harmony with reality. It is a principle. Truth is found in those realities that transcend a perceived experience."

"Reality," answered another star, "is only a resemblance to what is true. It exists independently of ideas concerning it."

"Ideals," said an even more distant star, "are the ultimate aims of any endeavor. They exist only in the imagination yet constitute the standard for all perfection. They are known only by the mind, and as such are the only true knowledge."

"Value," spoke an unseen star, "is that ideal which can create an emotional response. Value is its own means, and its own end. Value is intrinsic in nature, sometimes hiding behind reality and truth."

"All of these concepts are capable of rising beyond the fundamental attributes of human limitations," whispered another star, more quietly than the others. It was a whisper, but it came through loud and clear. "These are the concepts which through the dreams and imaginations of man control and direct his very existence. These are the fibers that combine to produce and give form to his dreams. These are the substance of his soul. It is through their dreams, through their souls, that these mortal beings are able to manipulate their lives."

Star-baby watched as obscure images floated among the whispers, with glimmers of light almost, but not quite, illuminating them to the point of recognition. The whispering stars seemed to be chanting, a mantra of sorts. She interpreted it to be a song of knowledge, and the knowledge seemed to pertain to life.

The whispers grew softer and the gentle winds intensified. The scant glimmers of light flickered less frequently and then were gone. Only the wind remained and in a low, hypnotic and melodic voice, it too began to speak to her.

"If one chooses, choices will always exist. Those choices must be made in accordance with basic individual and personal truths. Be assured though, the consequences are not limited in time. They hold a power forceful enough to influence a lifetime and all time, with regret or satisfaction. You can choose those ideals you wish to believe in or those you wish to reject. You can choose to believe in ultimate justice or you can create and find a justice in every action you take. You can believe in the vision and realities provided by your imagination, or you can ignore them as nothing more than that which you cannot see."

And then the wind too was silent.

Star continued to look around for the source of the voice but except for the stars, it was dark, and no one was around except her new stable mate. She had heard voices before that seemed to come to her on the wind, from the sky, even once from a turtle she had found lumbering across a pasture one afternoon. Other horses talked to her as well, so she wasn't really all that surprised that stars should speak.

It was what to do with the words that puzzled her. She had taken the initiative with Mia and Zack. They "heard" her, but didn't know it. They "understood" the words but didn't comprehend the origin. Now, things were moving in a different direction.

She had no problem communicating with the other animals who immediately congregated in her stall. All four dogs moved out of their dog houses and into the stall, where at night they pawed nests of wood shavings and made themselves as small and flat against the side walls as possible. The cats made small cat balls in the corners. Even the mice showed up periodically, keeping their distance from the cats who didn't even seem to know, or care, that they were there. Star-Baby didn't mind, though all these extra inhabitants did crowd and cramp her sleeping arrangements somewhat. She suggested some of them sleep with Bubba, but Bubba wouldn't have any of it. He wanted his space, and didn't want to share.

It was funny to her, the things that were important to the strange group of barnyard residents.

The dogs were most worried that someone might forget to feed them. They loved their food and looked forward to it all day long. They worried that it might rain, and they wouldn't be able to sleep in the sun. They worried that company would come, and they'd be locked up. And if anyone backed the car to the front of the house to load anything, they worried that the people were taking a trip. Then they worried all over again that they might not be fed on time, or at all.

The cats worried that a new cat or kitten would show up. They worried that the birds might eat their cat food. They worried about coyotes and mountain lions.

Bubba worried too, about whether or not the supply of hay in the hay shed was getting too low, whether his grain would be changed, whether the water would freeze. He lost track of time day-to-day, but could tell almost to the week when it was time for the farrier, or when the vet was due out to give shots and float teeth. He really worried about that.

Star-baby talked to all of them. She tried to calm their fears and doubts.

"Think about it. You're building too many walls that only have to come back down. Dig a little deeper. What are you really worried about? What's the worst that could happen?" she asked.

It was the wrong question, because she was told in no uncertain terms what they expected the worst to be.

Bubba too, spoke to her regularly. When not telling her what to do, where to graze, which pile of hay she could eat, and in general just bossing her around, he would tell her about his days as a ranch horse, a cow horse, a rodeo star. He had worked cattle, he could cut, he knew how to head those doggies out. He told her about the horrors at the children's camp. And even though he was a quarter horse gelding, he didn't seem to realize he had been gelded. That too, had been a new experience.

Bubba was full of ideas, and looked at the world in a way that was very different from how Star-baby saw it. Where Bubba was grounded, Star-baby was motion. One of the first things he had told her was to quit worrying. This from a horse who was always worried. He didn't realize at the time what she was worried about.

"It's like that rocking horse story, you know, about worry. Worry is just like a rocking' horse. It's something to do that can be a little comforting, but in the long run, just won't get you anywhere."

Good old Bubba.

Like many of the people Star-baby had observed, Bubba was all things. Endearing in his way, truly insufferable at times, sweet and sour, kind and angry, full of himself but not so full there wasn't room for need, or room for someone else.

Star-baby had stories and advice for Bubba as well. She liked Bubba. He was pragmatic, and practical, and never made a move he didn't have to make. When "the people" decided it was time to ride, he would make himself as scarce as possible in what was actually a fairly small area. He had the idea that up close, if he stood just so, because he couldn't see around it, he could hide behind a tree. And there he would stand, as still as the tree itself. It never worked, and he'd ultimately end up saddled and ridden. Still, on the occasions Star-baby was taken out by herself, by her new person, he didn't want to be left behind. On his own terms, he wanted to be included.

"Better decide, Bubba," she told him. "You can't have it both ways. Stay or go. Accept it or fight. First though, you better figure out which battles are worth fighting, why you're fighting them, and what outcome you're trying to achieve. You know the facts of it all won't go away just because you ignore them."

But, Bubba was a stubborn old soul, and wasn't a very good listener. Still, he heard everything, but without Star-baby's ability to communicate his thoughts, he kept it all inside, waiting, until it was his turn to act.

Now, for me, having my horse, well, in point of fact, two horses, but most importantly my own special horse, I reiterate, my horse, finally, a horse I could go out and ride at will, groom and brush and hug, feed and love, was still new and a little unbelievable. It was as if it all folded into a dream and I never wanted to wake up.

They say, "beware that which is just as you want it to be," but I never understood why. It's what I had always wanted, and it's the way I wanted things to stay. But things don't stay, they don't stay the same, and that's what it is about life, and dreams, they may or may not die, but they fade into each other where one becomes so much of the other that to define one means to lose one.

It was during one of those rides Bubba was actually able to avoid, just me and the Lovely and Talented Star-Baby, when something happened that would change the way I saw the world. Such a declaration should have trumpets and drum rolls and a heavenly chorus, but it was nothing like that. And, in a way, it was more.

It was one of several regular routes, this one along an unpaved road that led eventually to the Pedernales River. There were a couple of long, level places along the way to get in a few good gallops, on good days, a dead-on run.

We were moving pretty well, not yet full-out and not yet out of control, but as usual, getting there. It was time to slow down. Almost. The next turn in the road was blind. You couldn't see around it and neither could anyone coming from the other direction. That turn always made me nervous and here it was. And this is where it happened. In a way, this is where it started.

"Whoa!" Not from me. That "whoa" came from the sky above and the air around us and it was a voice I knew well.

My dad had been gone for eight years, but it was his voice all right that filled my head. The Lovely and Talented, for the first time in her life, stopped on a dime, sort of skipping herself into a full and complete stop. She stood there, ears pricked forward, blowing through her nostrils as I tried to work my way down her neck and back into the saddle. We just stood there, both of us shaking, while a large buck, a very large nine point buck came tearing through the overgrowth that made the corner so blind. He never slowed down and two-thirds of the way across the road, right about where we would have been, leapt high enough to clear the old barb wire fence at the other side. It was a disaster in the making.

The buck just kept going.

"You heard it too," I said to my beloved horse. "That, was my Father." And that's when she answered.

"It's a good thing he was watching. If you don't mind my saying so, you really shouldn't go so fast around that turn. Sometimes it's better to slow down when you can't see what you're doing. You'll still get where you're going."

This from the horse that had three speeds, one of which was, still. But the strange thing was, well, one of the strange things, it didn't strike me as odd that we were having a conversation until later. I could have been talking with anyone. No, I was still trying to figure out how we both heard my Father's voice. The first word that flashed into my mind was "miracle." Was it? Maybe it was what had to happen. And maybe it had to happen for reasons yet unknown.

All at the same time, Star-baby reached the realization that someone actually heard her. Heard and acknowledged without question. Finally. She had a lot to say.

And from then on, I had my hands very full. I also had to decide what to do with this new secret. Who in the world was going to believe that not only did my horse talk to me, but that my deceased Father had talked to us both? And, more, that we both heard him.

Star-Baby must have spent the night wondering what to do with her new ability to openly communicate, if only with one person. I know I did. I didn't say anything to anyone. There wasn't anything, at least anything plausible, to say. As far as I could see, there wasn't an explanation in the world for such enlightenment. At least I recognized that it wasn't the details that were important, it was that there had been such an interaction at all. Hadn't there been?

Should I test her, should I challenge her to prove herself? Would she? I was almost afraid to find out. I wanted it both ways, and only one outcome was possible. Was this what a miracle was? Was there even such a thing? Weren't miracles really just illusions, just forms of magic, something you could understand once you understood the tricks behind them? Weren't they?

Star-Baby saved me the trouble. She was more up than I for what was ahead.

As soon as I reached the tack room that next morning, I heard her. She had been waiting for me. She had a lot to say.

"You're troubled by this. You're apprehensive, hesitant, worried about what to do, what to say, who to tell, how to tell it. I wouldn't worry too much. No one will believe you anyway."

"Great, Star. That's really comforting. That makes it really easy."

"It's not supposed to be easy. It's just supposed to be. That's what makes it worthwhile. That's why you're here. That's why it's all here. And there. And there. And there. It's up to you to put it together. Here."

I wasn't sure I understood exactly what she meant by "there or here," but I was pretty certain it was more involved than standing there with a bucket of grain in my hand.

"Why me, Star? What am I supposed to do that's any different from anyone else?"

"Nothing. It's all the same. You're no different. Well, you're a little different. Sorry. And of course, here I am. I'm here with you. I'll do what I can to help, but I can't do it all. I can only lend a hand, or hoof, here and there, and only to the extent you help yourself. So now, you have to figure out what it is you're after, and believe it or not, you're getting close. You will probably be surprised too, when you discover that what you're after isn't all that different from what most of the human race is generally, unknowingly, yet blissfully in pursuit of.

"You were always told that everyone is created equal weren't you? The truth of it is that not everyone ends up on an equal footing. See, there's more to it than that. It's actually, and only, mortality that makes everyone equal. There it is. Out there to deal with, like it or not. It's what gives meaning to courage, pain, laughter, tears and love. Lucky for you, there's not enough wealth in the world to buy these things. They are just here to take. So grab them when you can, hold on to them, cherish them. You'll lose them soon enough."

She was in my head. She was in my thoughts and soul. She had been saving up for a very long time and she wasn't finished. Not by a long-shot. I was lost.

"It's a big universe. Life is big. Life is full of good and bad, success and failure, evil and kindness, doing the right thing at the right time, the right thing at the wrong time, and then turning around and doing the exact wrong thing at anytime. Life is unfair. And still, sometimes things work out the way one wants them to, whether that's the way they should work out or not. And, sometimes they don't. But, it's all we've got."

I had myself a really smart if unworldly horse.

Evidently, other people, for reasons I couldn't rationally identify, thought so too. It got so that every time we had friends over, heading out to the horses to see Star-Baby was first on everyone's schedule. Even before margaritas and martinis. The lovely and talented would glide over to the fence while each person in turn would have the chance to greet her and lightly touch her soft nose or cheek, sometimes palms held flat with the offering of an apple or carrot slice. I understood the need, the pleasure, the satisfaction, but after all, she was my horse. I was a little jealous of the attention she returned to others.

It was the same on the telephone. Family or friends called and before asking how I was, or about Husband or Daughters, it was almost always, "And how is the Lovely and Talented Star-Baby?"

And I always answered the same way. "Perfect," I would say.

"Star?" I asked one day while untangling and moisturizing her silky white mane. "What is this all about? Why are you here? How does this work? Is it about good and evil? Who are you? There's so much of everything, on every level, every subject, can any one act, good or bad, right or wrong, really make that much of a difference in today's world? How can it possibly?"

Her head was up, the flat of her cheek just about equal with my forehead. She rolled an eye down to look at me. She might have been thinking, forming her thoughts before she offered her wisdom, but the pause and look that went with it was more likely than not mostly for effect. Star had that affect on people, and worked it to her advantage.

"It's like stirring the sea. You make ripples, then waves, then the waves roll in. Crash. Boom. They crash against shorelines, they crash against rocks, beaches erode. But yes, there is change. Slow, steady, change. I'm just here trying to make a few waves.

"What I say, what others hear, it won't be the same for everyone. People by nature are divided, they are contentious. It's why there are so many disagreements on so many different levels. Still, overlooking what is not understood is actually pretty easy. Maybe not productive, but easy. And universally, it will never be understood in the same way or at the same time, so to make any kind of difference, it has to be said over and over and in different ways. And still, most of you guys won't even care. It doesn't matter. You'd be surprised how few actions, how few achievements, even those so small you would think no one would notice, at how little it takes to make a big difference in the order of this universe."

My life divided itself into before Star-Baby and after Star-Baby.

The motion of life moved on, sometimes shifting slightly, like the tide. Like Star's waves, it ebbed and flowed.

Breaking everything down to day-by-day, which isn't as simple as it sounds but is about as much as most of us can handle at one time, it seems we move through life in a never-ending tangle of have-to and want-to, right and wrong, yes and no, what has to come first, and why. Where are we headed, how do we know when we're there, and then what? What comes next, and then, the same questions start over again.

It was a question I once asked the Lovely and Talented Star-Baby as I mucked her stall. It was a question in passing, spoken out loud, more because the consequences of work, success or failure, and what either would ultimately mean, were constantly on my mind, than because I really expected an answer. "Where in the world are we headed? Why is this so hard? And then what?"

Star-Baby was contentedly crunching her grain, grinding it round and round, rolling her jaws, but paused long enough to answer.

"What would you do without me? Technically, that's three questions. They're not questions I can, or should answer, even for you, but questions you need to answer for yourself. Even then, the true meaning is impossible to judge, its destiny impossible to know. But here's what I will tell you.

"Some things in life just are. That's all. It's as simple as that and it's just the way it is. There are no directions to the

rules. Some things are just true, they are as they are, and because they are, there is no need to prove them. Right and wrong don't change. They have always been and will always be part of the greater truth. And, here's the great beauty of this truth—it too, just is. It just exists. And because it exists, in its own way, it touches each of us, changing our realities, and itself, every time. It's what makes it true. With us, because of us and even in spite of us. You'll see when you get there."

Oh Lord. Star just looked at me. She snorted. She blew. She nodded her head up and down, then shook it vigorously, leaving her mane haphazardly split on either side of her most beautiful and graceful neck.

"You know, like it or not, understand it or not, believe it or not, life isn't designed to accommodate you. It's meant to shatter you, and it does it very well. You know about the seeds, right? It's an old story. Look at the life of seeds. Unless the shell shatters, is destroyed, there's nothing. Just a little seed in a tough shell. Nothing grows, nothing lives, nothing happens. And then, the shell breaks open, the seed sprouts, and there's life again. Life to sustain life. There you go."

All this while mucking out a stall.

I didn't know where or how far things would go, what this horse was all about, but I knew for a fact that the journey would be remarkable. Extraordinarily incredible. It already was. I knew it would be a trip, and like it or not, believe it or not, I was only along for the ride.

The morning I met Star-Baby's pigeons was a morning like almost every other morning. It was 6:30 AM when I went out to feed. Not too hot yet, and the air was a sweet mix of yesterday's heat and the morning's freshness. There was a tangible hint of Sycamore mixed with Cedar. It was easy, and pleasant to breath it in. This day was no different from the one before, except for one thing. I opened the corral gate and turned to walk into Bubba's stall, when out flew two hell-bent, kamikaze, fat, purple-grey pigeons who had been roosting on the rafter in Star's stall.

"Pidge and Midge," simply stated Star-Baby. "You probably know why they're here."

"No Star. I don't have a clue as to why you have pigeons."

"Come on. They're the symbol of hope and peace and even innocence. They're one of the few things in the Bible that all four gospels agree on. Remember Noah and his Ark, how the pigeon went out and came back with an olive leaf? It's profound. The sign of better times to come, solid ground, and that olive leaf, just a sprig of hope but it can be enough. Isn't that what you're looking for? And while they're at it, they want to hang around and eat the grain Bubba dribbles under his feeder."

"Star, don't you mean doves? I thought Noah had doves, white doves."

"It's a story. Doves, ravens, pigeons, colors, they're all birds. The important thing is, they finally arrived. No olive leaf, but we already know what that's all about. Remember hope?

"See, you can't, you probably wouldn't even want to survive without hope. Maybe all it takes are just a few hopeful

signs, just a glimmer of hope. Without hope there would be no faith in the future, and without that, there's no power in the present. It's the essential ingredient of life. In fact it's probably the greatest need there is."

"But Star, hope isn't solid. It can't pay bills. It can't heal disease. If you ask me, it's really more like wishful thinking."

"Maybe, maybe not. The thing about hope is, it means going on hoping when things seem hopeless. If not, it's no virtue at all. When things are good, when the future is bright and truly hopeful, then hope is just a platitude. But when everything seems really hopeless, that's when hope becomes strength. That's when it keeps you going. Haven't you ever heard the saying, 'hope is hearing the melody of the future and dancing to it in the here and now?' "

"Never heard it."

"Now you have. Start dancing."

"You're making me crazy. Life's not a dance, it's a wrestling match." To myself, I wondered, what is it about hope, is there hope when there is no hope left? I wasn't about to ask Star-baby. Enough was enough. For now.

Yet, it was on this same day, that hope was suddenly justified and we unexpectedly and breathlessly found ourselves way further from the edge of the ever-present cliff. It was just a small triumph, a little success, but together it was all a pretty big thing.

Star-baby was right. Life was big. It was full of hope. It had to be.

Part Four

It's been asked whether the end is indeed as hard as the beginning? Is it even the end at all? Has there really been a beginning, or is it instead all a part of the continuum? What are the circumstances, what are the facts, what makes each story true, and what makes it true across time?

This and every other story ever told, has to end at some point for each of its characters, but it ends for each in a different place, in its own time, in its own manner. It ends, yet at the same time, it begins again. It ends, yet it doesn't. It's all old and it's all new, for each of us, in our own interpretation, our own time, our own explanation, in meeting, or trying to meet our own expectations, in coming to terms with our own justifications.

No matter what, according to Star-baby, we all leave in the middle of our stories.

Mia

Returning to an empty house, empty barns, an empty life had been hard. But she had stayed only long enough to pack up the few belongings she couldn't leave and wouldn't sell. Memories of childhood, family, horses, of another time, another life. It was an old familiar pain, back for an unwelcome visit. Words in her head that conjured up another, very different lifetime.

Mia loaded her memories in the Suburban and headed east. Wildmare Farm was sold and there was nothing there any longer of any substance that belonged to her. She drove for three days, and when she came to Leesburg, Virginia she stopped. There was no plan, just a piece of paper, a single destination with an unknown outcome, an ad requesting applicants to apply in person, and the deep need in her soul to be in a different place.

The long white fences that outlined the paddocks and arenas were well-kept. One, two and sometimes three horses grazed peacefully in each paddock. The long barn at the end of the rows of paddocks was large, open, and appeared to be well-lit in the dusky evening light. Mia stopped to watch before going in. It would be strange, living and working in someone else's dream. But it was work she knew and work she loved.

Gold Springs Farm in Leesburg was one of the top Dressage training facilities in the country. If Mia couldn't breed her Arabians, she could at least train other horses through the levels and disciplines of Dressage.

True to form, the job had been filled. The new instructor had already settled-in and made his place in the staff quarters. Mia would have been devastated but she was too exhausted from packing and the drive, from the trauma and life-altering changes of the last four weeks. It must have all shown on her face because the owner suggested she stay at least overnight. Gold Springs Farm maintained temporary quarters that were furnished and ready. Dinner was served at 8:30, after the horses were settled. Breakfast was at 6:30 if she cared to join them. Then, there were other farms nearby where she might find an opening.

Mia remembered what she had come to think of as "Stella's words." Of course, she knew they hadn't really been Stella's, that just could not have been so, but it was with Stella when they had come to her. Words of the value, or lack of value, of risk without danger, fame and fortune without the prospect of rejection. Mia had the idea that she was developing a very strong sense of values.

She only unpacked enough for the night. There was still an hour before dinner, an hour to explore, and that meant the barn.

The horses were magnificent. Mia offered to help with the blankets and feed, and the offer seemed appreciated. It was good to be around horses again. What she really wanted to do was ride.

The foreman watched as she talked to the foals and yearlings. He admired the easy way she had. He admired her as well.

The next morning Mia was up early, well before sunrise. Again, she went to the barn, and again, she spent the next hour moving among the babies and yearlings. It reminded her of happier times, of times with Stella and the grey mare, times she desperately wanted back. She washed up before breakfast, where she would offer her thanks for the room and say goodbye.

"If you would still like a job, it seems we need someone to manage the younger horses, work with them, get them ready for training. Would you be interested?"

Would she be interested? Was she still alive?

Life was moving forward once again. Mia threw herself into the new job. She enjoyed the people and she enjoyed the work. She suspected Peter, the foreman at Gold Springs, had arranged for the job. He was all business around the horses, but after hours, he liked to sit and talk or share a bottle of wine over a game of chess or poker. It was all in giving and receiving companionship, and was done with a wicked-dry sense of humor.

But most of all, Mia enjoyed the horses. And, there was one, a special yearling, a one-year old dark grey mare. Perseus, named after one of the largest constellations in the northern hemisphere, reminded her dearly of Stella.

Mia had made "Percy" her special project. She expected great things of this foal, and it was now her personal mission to see how far she could go.

A year went by, and then another. Time was smooth, seamless. It was as if time stood still and moved too fast to follow, all at the same time.

Mia had begun riding Percy. She had her own method that was nothing more than hard work and patience. There were instructors and trainers who cut corners, putting a horse in a mechanical frame, at the same time short-cutting the basics. To Mia that was the equivalent of taping the horse's mouth shut. Horses had to be able to tell you where the problems were. She would never suffocate their unique ability to move, on their own, in their own way, in lightness and harmony.

Mia was establishing solid basics, reviewing and going back to them each time she rode Percy. Her work wasn't unnoticed. Both Peter and Gold Springs' owners saw how she always worked her with long and low stretches, always on command, in all three gaits, never falling on the forehand or losing rhythm and balance. Mia knew that without this ability no horse can perform to its full potential. She knew that stretching taught horses self-carriage and how to become independent of the rider's hands, at the same time building a strong top-line and powerful hind quarters, making it possible for the horse to step further under itself, round its back and raise its withers, allowing it to free its shoulders. She encouraged each horse to be its best self. And so they were.

It's what she had worked for and wanted for Stella. Even after the time that had passed, Mia thought about Stella every day, comparing Stella and Percy, wondering what had become of her old horse. And at the same time, thanking her for what she had given, remembering, always remembering how Stella had somehow helped her through a period she doubted she would have been able to navigate on her own.

Another year passed. Mia had worked with Percy for almost four years. They had moved from the Training, or Introductory Level, through Fourth Level, which was actually the fifth stage, in what she considered record time. It spoke extraordinarily well of the type of horse Percy was becoming.

The USDF, United States Dressage Federation show in Lexington at the Kentucky Horse Park was one of the biggest in the world of Dressage. Gold Springs was taking six horses. Mia would show Percy at Fourth Level.

Mia and Percy worked perfectly, straight and aligned, in a synchronization that was a dance in itself. Each horse in the competition was a potential champion, but in Percy, Mia knew there was that spark that defined the word. The judges tended to agree.

All the horses from Gold Springs did well and as the events closed, Percy was on her way to becoming a nationally recognized champion.

The next year was spent showing and training. When Percy and Mia returned to Lexington in 2005 it would be as Prix St. George contenders. Mia fully expected within the next four years to show Percy at the Grand Prix level.

She would never understand how, or why, she arrived where she was, but Mia was grateful. It was a more simple life, yet at the same time, it was the life she knew she was meant to live. Somehow, and with some amount of grace and faith intact, she had moved on from her losses at Wildmare Farm. She still thought about the grey mare, and she thought often enough about Stella to the point that it felt Stella was still with her, in spirit and soul, in almost everything she did. It was almost as if Stella was guiding her to some unknown destiny.

Mia and Peter were engaged. They were happy and planned to marry over the Holidays.

In late 2005, Percy won the Prix St. George Championship honors. In 2006, it was Intermediare I. In 2009, with Peter and Noel, their Christmas baby watching, Mia and Percy took top honors at the USDF Grand Prix level. Percy was amazing, and as Mia received the medal, her thoughts flashed again to Stella, to how, "a change of heart changes everything." Mia's heart had changed. It belonged to Peter and Noel and Percy. Her thanks and gratitude belonged to so many more.

Afterwards, in the barn, wrapping Percy's legs, a task she insisted on performing herself, Mia sensed rather than heard someone behind her. She stood and turned.

"I thought that was you. Looks like we've both come a long way."

At first she didn't recognize him, he was older, he had changed. He was another person from the one she had briefly known. But, he was also the same. It was the boy who had helped her, the person who bought Stella at the ill-fated auction so long ago. Another lifetime ago.

"Stella. Do you still have Stella? How is she?"

Zack shook his head. "I got accepted to the veterinary program in Fort Collins. I sold her to a nice lady and her little girl, for my first semester's tuition. I've lost touch. I live in Lexington now, specialize in treating performance horses. My contract rotates the USDF shows where I'm on call. You obviously know what those shows are like."

Mia didn't know how to take the news. She hadn't expected to ever see either Zack or Stella again, but it had settled her on some nameless level to believe she'd known where Stella was. Now, she could be anywhere.

"You know, that horse, I changed her name to Star, I hated to sell her. There was something about her that just wasn't quite what you expected from a regular horse. A feeling. There was something about her that was a little unnerving, a little intimidating almost frightening, you know? You'll probably think I'm a little crazy, but she was in a peculiar way, more than a horse. In another way, a bigger way still, she was more than human. In a funny way, and I'm not at all sure how, I think you could say she changed my life. And, even though she's no longer physically in it, even after all this time, she's still a big part of it."

Mia looked at Zack as if he'd just sprouted appendages and an extra eye.

"You too?"

It occurred to Mia that this was perhaps how real life dreams are supposed to go. Sometimes you lose track of what's important, sometimes you just don't know, and sometimes they are too elusive to hang on to. But then, sometimes they just drag you around before eventually depositing you exactly where you needed to be all along.

Richard

Poor Richard. Things didn't work out so well in San Francisco. The Gretchen project ended in divorce after only a little more than a year. What did he expect?

Well, for starters, he'd expected someone to take care of him, be there for him, be there when he needed someone there. As it turned out, that wouldn't have been Gretchen. He'd expected someone to see him for who he was, for what he had to offer. That could have well been Gretchen.

Richard hadn't brought that much to the relationship. He'd brought his charm, his good looks, and his talent for numbers, as long as they involved other peoples' money. He'd brought his baggage as well.

Richard had liked the flat in Sausalito. He liked the view and he liked the location. There wasn't a horse or bale of hay in sight. It was just across the bay, about as close to downtown San Francisco as you could get. Trendy and pricey. And that said it all.

Gretchen had picked out the furnishings. All white and off-white, right down to the thick carpet. No place for footprints, certainly not mud, or even the evidence that anyone lived or walked there. Even the kitchen utensils, cookware and dishes were white. It was Gretchen's favorite color. That too, said it all.

Richard had been puzzled, then slowly and almost intuitively, he had finally figured out that what Gretchen liked best about him when they first met was that he was married, to someone else. She'd married him anyway, which was good for her when she needed to use the marriage as an excuse. And as the excuses grew in number, they also grew in creativity. Richard had even used some of them himself.

That had been one very long year.

After the divorce Richard had actually played with the idea of calling Mia. Neither had seen any reason to stay in touch after the joke of a settlement. He wondered sometimes what she was doing. He had gone so far as to dial their old number, but it had been disconnected. There was no new listing in Amarillo or anywhere else in Texas. He'd given up easily.

Instead, he updated his resume and applied for a job with a rapidly growing real estate development company. Two years later, when the company filed for bankruptcy, it was Richard who had been held accountable. He should have seen it coming, but somewhere along the way, he'd lost his edge.

The firm had been almost too eager to hire him based on his pumped-up qualifications. No need for reference checks? He remembered thinking that it was either the most laid-back company in history, or the most naïve. He was wrong on both counts. It didn't take much hindsight for Richard to figure out that it was a set-up from the beginning, and that as far as he could see, there was no way he could ever prove it. No email or paper trail existed, other than the one with his fingerprint signature all over it.

His reputation was in shatters, and he was facing criminal charges. Contractors, creditors and attorneys were out for moral blood. After the example made of the Enron mess, he didn't stand a chance in hell. While on the subject, he hoped to hell his attorney knew what he was doing. How in the world had he come to this?

He was a fork stuck in the middle of some lost road, at a turning point with no place to turn and no one to turn to.

It was here that Richard again found his thoughts turning more often to Mia. He assumed she had recovered from the loss of her marriage, her farm, her horses, the life she had known and loved. At the time, that hadn't meant anything to him. Now, it did. And in understanding that recognition he acknowledged she was stronger than he had ever been. She had lost all she cared about, and he hoped, somehow knew, that she had moved on.

Knowing Mia, he felt she had to have moved forward. It was who she had always been, always moving, onward. On the other hand, he had come to realize that he had never really cared about anything, and that said a lot about how he came to be exactly where he was.

But he didn't really know any of this to be true because he had left. Like the coward he knew himself to be, he had just left. He did remember that on the day he'd closed that door for good Mia hadn't yelled, cursed or thrown anything. She had always had too much class for temper tantrums.

To his back she had said calmly, almost too calmly, "Richard, the world is full of grace and truth. And while there are such things as absolute ideals and absolute grace, you'll never resolve the tension between the two. You'll never measure up. Most of us don't have to. We just have to try. But you, all you care about is power, your power, and what you don't see is that no matter how well-intentioned, power has the overriding ability to cause suffering. It's love, it's vulnerable love that absorbs that suffering. And of that, you know nothing."

She had surprised him. It must have made an impression because he remembered it still. Where had that come from? Mia had been all about the horses. It was as if she was in her own world with them. Had she really understood so much about him, more even than he knew of himself? It was a Mia he hadn't known.

She had been right about his need for power. It's what had gotten him into this mess. But he didn't see it getting him out. How was that for a contradiction?

His attorney advised him to turn state's evidence and plea bargain.

"Agree to plead guilty or no contest in exchange for concession from the prosecutor. Maybe we can get the original charges dismissed or at the very least, limit the punishment. They've already charged you with the most extreme counts they feel they can prosecute. Your only choices at this point are between the certainty of accepting sentencing for a much less serious charge, being found innocent on all charges, or the uncertainty of a jury trial in which you might be found not guilty, but which also carries the risk of being found guilty."

Richard's head swam with the implications.

"If you have information which would help in prosecuting a broader or more significant matter, like what the developers have done with the profits, and why, I think we can get the prosecutors to agree to reduced charges or sentencing on your part. Maybe drop the charges all together. We don't know yet what they have. The evidence may not be enough to convince a jury of your guilt. But maybe it is. With a plea bargain, we can avoid the chance that you may be found guilty of the more damaging charges. For the other side, the prosecutor will avoid the possibility of you being found not guilty.

"Everyone wins. Sort of. At least, you will probably stay out of prison. Just think, Richard. You must know something."

Richard had protested, saying there was nothing he could offer. He was the victim. He didn't know anything.

Surely he suspected something, suggested the attorney. Hadn't there been signs, hadn't any little bells gone off in Richard's head, not that he should make anything up, of course not that, but couldn't he think of anything at all they could use to bargain?

So he had. Richard had suddenly thought of quite a bit. He thought, he analyzed, he deliberated and he justified. As far as he knew, none of it was true, but they couldn't prove that either. At least it placed the blame where it belonged. There was a kind of justice in that. He could live with his perjury knowing it was for the right reason. And if it kept him out of prison at the same time, well, that made it all the more justifiable.

He blamed it on the system. The whole plea bargain system had exerted strong pressure on him to plead to a crime he knew he did not commit. He knew too, that the outcome of that plea bargain was a direct result of the negotiating skills and shark-like personal demeanor of the overpaid defense lawyer he had hired.

With just a nudge, a little bend in time, a slight warp to his thoughts, the lies became truth.

There were many things Richard knew he didn't want to do, but he really didn't want to go to prison. As it turned out, his plea bargain strategy worked. He was fined for his alleged part in the land scheme, he was placed on probation, he was prohibited from holding certain jobs. But he knew all of this ahead of time. He'd had time to prepare.

Even with his reputation ruined, he too, could now move forward. He had been set up, but in turn, he had set up his own revenge. He had been had, but so had they, all of them, including the attorneys who hadn't been nearly as interested in justice as in their own fees. He could never get even, he would never have the life he wanted or felt he deserved, but he had the freedom to pursue it.

What is it about us, any of us, that makes forgiveness so hard? It was a question Richard had tried to answer after the trial when he thought about what had happened to him, and why it had happened. Forgiveness was hard. And to move forward, his counselor told him he had to "forgive to get past his anger." Richard wasn't in a forgiving frame of mind, but he also didn't know exactly whom it was he had to forgive.

He knew enough to know, whether he liked it or not, that everything that had happened had been his own fault. It had been his greed, his selfishness, his self-importance and self-indulgence that had gotten him where he was. The word, "narcissistic" had been tossed around. He was to blame. Hard to admit, but if he was honest with himself, that's the way it was.

Maybe he should just forgive himself and be done with the whole question? The more he thought about it, the more Richard decided that was the answer.

Richard and Gretchen had divorced well before the entire mess. She had gone to Europe, remarried, and divorced again. Richard didn't know the details, and didn't really care. She had come back to California, and during the preliminary hearing, indictment, arraignment and plea, had become more attentive, almost supportive. She had offered to help with his legal fees, an offer Richard had been quick to accept. He suspected she enjoyed the somewhat seedy spotlight, but the reasons for her renewed attention didn't bother him as much as being alone had, and not nearly as much as being almost broke had.

Unfortunately, or maybe fortunately for Richard, as soon as it was over and the headlines died down, Gretchen was gone again. This time he didn't mind so much. He was almost glad to see her go. He didn't pursue the cause. He was ready to move on, in some direction, on some new course, and with Gretchen he could finally see that there was no permanence of any manner. There was no substance.

He had told her there were no hard feelings. Actually, there was nothing. As long as he was in the forgiving spirit, himself included, whether it was even his to forgive, he decided he should get the most from it he could.

"I forgive you, Gretchen. For whatever we've done to, or because of each other, I forgive you and your part in all of this mess."

It hadn't been so hard, in part because he didn't truly think Gretchen understood what it was he was saying. But, it was done.

Richard had a new job, in marketing, for a software firm. He had no access to the company's accounts, nothing to do with finance. Fine by him.

He had passed the historic Golden Gate Park Stables in San Francisco on his way to work the day before. The stables had closed in 2001 after a 130-year history because of lack of funding. Now, the Stable Foundation hoped to revive and develop the dilapidated structures into a top class riding facility, a cause Richard knew Mia would approve of. Mia and her causes. Maybe this was a cause, even one that involved horses, or because it involved horses, that he could do something about. Maybe it would make up for just a small part of what he had done, what he had set in motion.

The closing of the stables didn't keep riders out of the park. He had watched as a young woman cantered past him on a large grey horse. The horse's head had been up, nostrils wide, mane blowing back toward the rider, whose eyes had been filled with the thrill and love of the ride.

He had thought of Mia, riding her beloved grey mare. He thought of Mia talking excitedly about the grey mare's daughter Stella, and her great promise. He thought of those horses, and Mia, with a fondness he hadn't before acknowledged or even known. He truly hoped she was happy. He hoped she was with horses somewhere.

He hadn't understood it before, all the things Mia talked about when she talked about horses, but that scene in the park opened his eyes, made his heart pound, made the blood rush to his head, made his hands clench the steering wheel in a grip that turned his knuckles white, made him realize there was just something about a horse that was hard to define. It was grace. It was strength. It was a nobility that would serve a man well if he would let it. Was it indeed too much, too late, or perhaps, not enough too soon?

Gretchen

Lord knows it wasn't about money. She had plenty of that. She hadn't known how much Richard would enjoy spending it though. What Gretchen had thought she found in Richard was an excuse, an easy way to live the life she wanted to live. What she found was nothing of the sort. It never occurred to her that she should have known better. It never occurred to her that she should share some of the blame for all that had happened. That wasn't who she was.

Gretchen was a woman who did things her way, when it suited her. The rest of the time, she did things her way. She always had, she'd always gotten away with it, and she didn't intend to change. From the time she was a little girl, to her first marriage, to her first divorce, to Richard and after Richard, what was good for Gretchen, was good. What was not good for Gretchen, was bad. She knew she was selfish and self-centered, and she didn't care. She liked herself anyway, that way. Black and white, good and evil, right and wrong, yes or no, it was all the same to her as long as she came first and as long as she was satisfied.

That had been the problem with Richard. While he was married to Mia he had been fun. It had been an adventure. The adventure went south almost as soon as they had married and moved to San Francisco. Richard stopped being fun. He had needs. And for Gretchen, that meant her needs weren't being met.

Thank God for pre-nups. It had been as easy to get out of that marriage as it had been to get into it. There had been no profit in it, but it hadn't really cost her either.

Richard had complained that, "it left him with nothing. How could she leave him? After all he'd given up, all he'd done for her?"

He hadn't understood anything about her at all. After all, he kept the BMW, the stereo system, and the cat. What more did he think he was entitled to? What more did he want?

After Richard, Gretchen had traveled in Europe. It was the right season, and it only made sense to put some distance between them. She met and married and divorced an Italian businessman. Pre-nuptial agreements in Italy weren't quite as iron-clad as in the states. She had expected to come out ahead, again, but was surprised when it came to light that her new husband wasn't exactly who she thought he was. It seemed he had planned the same course of action as she, and he intended to make it pay off.

Lucky for Gretchen, his first wife, the one he hadn't bothered to divorce before he married her, got involved, and that put an end, more or less, to the question of who would profit.

When she returned to San Francisco, the papers had been full of Richard's indictment. Gretchen always saw things in terms of other people's failures, so naturally she wondered how Richard could have made such a mess of things in just a few years?

She was sure he had been glad to see her. At least he was glad to see she was going to help. It had been exciting, sitting in the courtroom, watching the proceedings. She'd never visited anyone in prison, and wondered if that opportunity too, would present itself if Richard went to trial and was found guilty.

But she didn't get the chance.

And she was more than a little surprised to find out that once the entire matter was over, Richard seemed fine without her. He didn't seem to care if she stayed or left. It was as if that part of his life had ended. No one was finished with her until she said so. Who did he think he was? Where did he think he would be without her?

And where was Gretchen? What was next? She could go back to her real estate business, but after she'd left for Europe, her clients had found new alliances. She would have to start over if that was what she intended to do.

Gretchen liked to do things the easy way, and starting from scratch wasn't easy. She'd done that once and with a helpful settlement and contacts from her first marriage and divorce, had been successful. But now, she didn't have those advantages, and now, she didn't like the odds.

Looks were one thing, but there were lots of "looks" out there, and working hers to her advantage was another thing entirely. She needed to put them to work while she was at her prime. She needed to pull out the stops. And, she needed prospects, she needed an angle. Her approach was calculated. Research the upcoming fundraising events. Research the single men who habitually attended those events. Choose one. Attend the right function. Target the right guy. The rest was easy. It was what she did best.

And it worked. Sort of.

He was handsome. He was connected. His name was always in the society columns and everyone who was anyone recognized it. He seemed to appear at every event, at least every event where Gretchen was present. It never occurred to her that his game was her own.

She found out too late. So did he. The joke was on them, and it was cosmic in scale.

In husband number four she met her match. It seemed they were stuck with each other. There was nothing financially for either to gain. They could call it quits then and there, or stick it out long enough to save face. Both opted for saving face. Besides, they told each other, they were both attractive, they liked fun and traveled in the right circles, and they definitely wanted the same things. They were attracted to each other. How bad could it be?

As it turned out, they were both equally surprised.

Gretchen was eight months pregnant, and husband number four was delighted. Gretchen was rather disgusted with herself, but there was always plastic surgery to fix any permanent damage. Besides, it meant husband number four now had a job to do. He had to take care of her and their pending progeny. Gretchen was again the center of someone's attention. Now that they were a family, there was more to consider than the party circuit.

Husband number four seemed up for the challenge and turned out to be quite successful at his job as an account manager with a healthcare technology group. The money was nice. It was very nice. Gretchen on the other hand, turned out to be a natural mother. They were able to hire a day Nanny, which meant Gretchen had time for the gym and lunch with the girls at least twice a week. Little Matthew was a good baby, liked his naps, laughed easily and hardly cried. He was loveable, accommodating and easy.

The same wasn't true for the twins, who followed sixteen months later, or the second set of twins thirteen months after that.

Four more babies in just over two years, and they were not easy babies. They were demanding, challenging, difficult and loud. There were so many of them. Five babies under four years of age. What had she done?

Gretchen found the pounds harder to lose. She had no time to herself, no time for exercise, no time for massages, manicures or hair. Husband number four did what he could, he was as supportive as he could be, but his job demanded he spend more and more time away. The company was growing. The promotions kept coming. As much as he wanted to be home with his family, his only means to support them was to be on the road.

Gretchen was envious. Gretchen was trapped and saw no way out. Her big plans for a big life were shrinking, and with them, the person she had always thought herself to be.

So she decided to approach it all from inside, from her strengths, from where she was now. Her hunger for self-indulgence too, played a large part. Too much work? Too much to handle? Overwhelming? You're not alone. It was the ad for her life, an ad made in heaven.

What do we really learn from each other? What can we learn? Surely something of each encounter must mean something.

Gretchen thought of Richard, not especially fondly, but of how he had overcome adversity, how he had kept the faith when things had seemed blackest. If he could do it, so could she.

Gretchen didn't know it, hadn't planned it, and hadn't even acknowledged it, but found herself all the same at the intersection of the spiritual and material world, looking for vision and balance and harmony between moral and ethical laws. And there it was.

The "Harbor Center" she set up was there for women with the means to take advantage of it. It offered a refuge, a time out. It offered a gym, day spa, day care, salon, restaurant and bar. Something for everyone, everyone with money. For Gretchen, it offered once again, on a new scale, prestige. With five young children, she was an instant expert in what women needed. She was their new spokesperson. She was back in what she had come to think of as "the game." But, the rules had somehow changed, were still a little vague, yet in some indefinable way, she intuitively knew it was to be a better game. How many lives would be touched, and then touch others?

All of a sudden, she was back on top, but she was not the same old Gretchen. She was a changed Gretchen. She didn't know why, but there was something about the new Gretchen that was a response, or perhaps a reaction, to what was missing in the old Gretchen.

She remembered Richard's "forgiveness." At the time she didn't know what was meant, where it had come from, what had been his reasons behind such an idea. Mercy? Amnesty? Pardon? Or perhaps it was all about his own effort to move on.

But he had been strong enough to make the overture and she was strong enough to acknowledge it.

It worked for her.

Backhoe Operator, Jim Bob

His mother had told him early on and often that with a fancy name like James Robert he would do big things. Perhaps it was unfortunate, perhaps not, but she was the only one who had ever called him James Robert. To the rest of the world he was Jim Bob. Just Jim Bob.

Jim Bob had always been his own person. He'd grown up hard, and he'd grown up fast. His daddy had left when he was six, and that had left him, his alcoholic mother, and three younger sisters all alone. Jim Bob was the oldest by two years. Maybe his parents should have stopped there, but they hadn't. The babies kept coming, and so had the beatings, maybe that was why his mother stayed pregnant, and then all of a sudden, his father was gone. One night he was there, hitting on Jim Bob, the next morning he wasn't.

Jim Bob had wondered where he had gone, what had caused him to leave so suddenly, but he hadn't really cared. He'd been more relieved than anything.

There had been talk. More than the usual "another woman." Everyone in town already knew there had been lots of other women. Since he hadn't left before, why now? And, why didn't he take the car? It was still there in the driveway. Yet, no one seemed to care that he was gone, not care enough to ask questions. Most people were just thankful to know he was gone.

Jim Bob almost graduated high school, had come within months, but there had been the incident in the gym. He'd tried to help, to step in and even up the sides, but somehow it had all ended up on him. The kid he'd tried to help had been too scared to understand Jim Bob was on his side, too scared, of something, to ever say anything about it. The other kid, the one who'd started it all, had found in Jim Bob a scapegoat for the mess he'd created. Jim Bob never did find out whose knife it was, he only knew it wasn't his. All the same, he'd been expelled.

He cared, but then he didn't really. It was pretty much what his life had come to. He'd been alone with himself for so long, this was really not that different. He knew he needed to do something though, but not just yet. He wanted to have some fun first.

Although he had worked odd jobs in high school, he had only saved enough money for about two weeks of fun. At the same time he had discovered that having fun on your own isn't really that much fun. Drinking alone, getting a little too drunk and then fighting alone, with no one to take your back.

When he'd gotten the job with the construction company it had meant more money than he'd ever known. Seven dollars an hour. That was something. And the great thing was, all he had to do was drive a backhoe around all day and move stuff. Dirt, stumps, concrete. He was finally doing big things after all. Who needed an education to do that?

This time he saved his money. His mother was gone. Not dead, but gone into drink. So, gone. One sister really was gone, somewhere. No one had seen or heard from her in over three years. The other two were home sometimes, sometimes not. They didn't seem to need him anymore. He guessed he didn't need them either, although sometimes he missed them, missed having some sort of family.

After a few years there was no reason to stay in that little hick town. If he could make money with a backhoe there, he could make more in a bigger city. It was time to seek opportunity, time to make his way.

Amarillo was big enough. Jim Bob felt right away that he fit in. He found an apartment, and a job. He was making $14 an hour. That seemed good enough for Tina, who managed the office.

Tina was divorced with two kids. They were nice kids, and Jim Bob once again liked having someone to take care of. He liked being able to talk to those kids, tell them things he thought they should know. He felt they sort of looked up to him, he wasn't sure why, but he knew he liked it.

Occasionally when he had dinner at Tina's he would take the kids, Dicky, an eight year-old, blond boy with black glasses, and Cathy Ann, a six year-old red-headed sprite, a small gift. Nothing elaborate, but always appreciated. He felt the beginnings of a family were emerging.

Jim Bob and Tina married sixteen months after they first met in the construction office and over the next five years, had two more kids of their own.

He was good at his job and had been promoted to foreman. He still drove the backhoe but not all the time anymore. Depended on the job.

The day after one of the biggest storms Amarillo had seen on record, with rainfall totals and damage estimates splashed all over the front page of the morning paper, he'd been sent to the fair grounds. Lightening had struck two horses and they needed to be hauled off, immediately.

And there he was, doing his job, operating the backhoe the exact same way he'd done for twelve years, when some kid holding a horse on a lead comes up and starts telling him how to do it. It didn't sit well. And it was then, out of the blue clear sky and all of a sudden, he'd heard it.

"If you don't understand it, it's an easy thing to overlook. It's easy to get it wrong."

"What?"

"This is not your time. It's not about you, not directly, but you are and will always be a part of it. Your actions create greater actions and are really all of the same part."

The words were a surprise to Jim Bob. No one had spoken, but he had clearly heard. He'd forgotten about his anger over being told how to do his job. He looked at the horses on the ground and the woman grieving for them, and he knew his job now was not just to remove the horses but to do it with a care that was strange to him.

For the rest of his life, Jim Bob would remember those words. Without even realizing how or when it happened, he would make choices that reflected those greater actions, and a greater time. He overlooked nothing and took nothing for granted.

That night he stopped on his way home and bought flowers for Tina. It was an extravagance, and a surprise to both of them, but for some reason, he felt thankful to have someone to take flowers to. She was touched. And for this feeling, she was thankful. Life still held surprises. Jim Bob hadn't told his wife about his day, it wasn't something he knew how to share, not through words. Something of them was changed, something they knew nothing about, something positive, encouraging and far-reaching.

He had changed. In the course of a day, he was not the same man. He didn't know how and he didn't know why, but he knew he was a better man, and because of it, his family was a better family, his kids were better kids, and their lives were better lives. It was a debt he somehow intended to repay, a gift he would someday pass on. But at the time Jim Bob knew none of this.

Zack

School had been hard, and at the same time, it had been the easiest thing he had ever done. It had filled deep holes and it had answered unasked and unresolved questions. It had been everything Zack had expected and needed. The years had gone by quickly and almost too easily. Zack had excelled.

He still remembered the pride he felt when he bought his first stethoscope. He had listened to his heart, and every animal's heart he could find to listen to. It was music to his ears. It was a good memory.

There were other memories too, some good, some with bad outcomes, and some scarier than he could have imagined. One such memory would stay with him always. It was one of the memories imprinted on his life. It was an event of lost control and good outcome. Not a miracle, in the sense he understood the word, but an event of success.

Colonel Klink was a big, almost 17-hand bay, 14 year-old quarter horse housed at the school for students to practice on. Splinting, floating teeth, exams, shots, drawing blood. It's a good thing he was a good-natured beast. Zack knew most horses were not that docile.

Zack was in his last 14 months of school and was just beginning his clinical rotation in equine medicine. When not with the instructor and fellow students, he tried to make time to sort of do his own rounds, a time when he would visit the horses, just to check on them, and if the truth were known, because he missed being around them. It was such a time when he noticed Colonel Klink shaking his head, a whistling sound coming through his nostrils. It was almost as if he were struggling to breathe. Zack pulled out his scope, but couldn't get it up the horse's nose. Something was blocking his nasal passages. What had the Colonel gotten into?

Zack knew this was beyond his experience, and paged one of the instructors and staff vet. After explaining the symptoms, and the blockage of the nasal passages he had to admit he didn't know where to go next. "Could he have broken something in his nose?" Zack had asked.

His instructor had smiled at that, and then looked at Colonel Klink as if he knew almost exactly what to look for. After the X-rays he pulled Zack over and said, "Look right here, Zack. Tell me what you see." Looking carefully he had blurted out, "it looks like golf balls. How could he have gotten golf balls way up there?"

"They're sinus cysts," the instructor explained. "Unusual in a horse his age, but it happens. Unfortunately, as I'm sure you know, the only way to remove them is surgery. What is your schedule tomorrow?"

Zack thought back to his clinical pathology and clinical radiology classes in his second semester and remembered studying sinus cysts, but he had never seen one.

Zack had never seen so much blood. During the surgery Colonel Klink had been transfused with literally gallons of blood.

The trachea, or windpipe, is a round and firm tube of cartilage, allowing air to pass from the mouth down the neck to the lungs. During the surgery, a stainless steel trachea tube was placed into Colonel Klink's windpipe about six inches below the throat, where air could enter his lungs through the tube rather than his nostrils, which were packed with gauze.

"Now, have you changed a trach tube before?" asked the instructor, "because this is going to be your job with this procedure." Zack had not.

"It's not that difficult."

Zack had been shown how to insert two small metal pieces and then how to rotate them into a locked position. He had been instructed to do it twice a day to keep the mucus from clogging, or the Colonel wouldn't be able to breathe. The scary part came when he was warned, that when the old trach tube came out, he only had about a minute to get the new one back in place, and that during that time the horse couldn't breathe. Zach would literally hold the horse's life in his hands.

"It's easy, you can do it," the instructor had said.

When it was time to change the trach tube for the first time   Zack had been nervous, and he had been alone. The schedule called for the switch to be made at 1 a.m.   The old tube came out easily. He immediately placed the tapered end of the new tube into the same insertion space. It wouldn't go in. He pressed harder, which resulted in moving the wind pipe to the side. He tried again. Now the not quite so docile Colonel Klink was trying to breathe and no air was getting in without the tube.

Zack tried again. By now the sweat was rolling from his forehead into his eyes, stinging them. "Be calm," he told himself. "You have to do this." Clearing the panic from his mind, and the sweat from his eyes, he tried again. The first part was in. The second piece went in and he locked them together. Colonel Klink drew a deep breath.

It was only then that for some reason Zack thought of Star, and how it already seemed forever ago when she had predicted, in her interminable way, his future.

"You'll stumble and you'll fall, but you were created for success. Be glad of the gift you have been given. It's one of the layers of your soul."

It had taken Zack awhile to recover from the realization that he had almost killed his first patient.

Zack's classes had been and were difficult but because he so loved the material, he found himself immersed in it. It took on a life of its own and swallowed him with it, but he didn't care. He was happy. He should have realized sooner that there was more to life than just existing, and that sometimes life itself, without reason, good, bad, expected or unexpected, provides unforeseen and unanticipated opportunity. That opportunity presented itself in the form of Nora.

Nora was a student in Zack's equine breeding management class. She too had a deep love for horses, and she too intended to make their welfare her life's work. Zack thought she was the most beautiful woman he had ever met.

It took a few classes before he worked up the nerve to ask her to go for a coffee with him. Over that coffee they discussed their mutual love of horses, how they arrived at Fort Collins, how they were fulfilling a lifelong dream. They found how similar and how different their lives were. They talked about past relationships, family, goals and aspirations. They were married three months later.

Zack marveled at how easy it had been, how easy they were together. It was nothing like with Charlene. Nora not only shared his dreams and passions, but she cared about his needs and understood and fully supported his expectations of life. It was what she wanted for herself as much as she wanted it for him.

How did he get so lucky? What had he done right? Had this been where his life was headed all along? But Zack knew neither life, or the answer to his question, was that easy. It was not a mystery to solve as much as a direction, a path to take. His had been long and winding to this point.

Zack thought back often to his one-sided conversations with Star. He wished he could share them with Nora, but he didn't know how to tell anyone that he thought his horse might have talked to him. More importantly, directed him. He didn't, in fact, really believe it himself, at least not in the sense that it might be real. What might exist in his head might take a lot of explaining, and he wasn't sure he knew how to go about it, or if he should.

But now, his life was finally his own. He felt that with Nora anything, even everything was possible. He knew too, that such security didn't come easily, and it certainly did not come with guarantees. But he was happily in search of it and that in itself was good enough. They say life is a comedy to those who think and a tragedy to those who feel. But in reality, Zack well-knew it is both.

He had called Charlene to tell her the news. It was the first time he had called her in almost three years. They had both moved on. Charlene sounded happy with her life, and Zack was glad for her.

James had told him about Charlene's marriage to the New Orleans urologist. Charlene hadn't bothered. She had married just over a year after Zack left. He knew it was what she had needed, that it was more than he had been able, or willing to give her. Stability and at the same time freedom, and in her mind, a sort of prestige. It's how Charlene defined herself.

As they talked, Zack felt a sense of loss, but it wasn't the loss of something he was particularly sad to lose. It was the loss of what had been a part of who he had been for a long time, but not a part he wanted back. It was a large part of who he had been, but no element of who he was now, or who he would ever be again. With that sense of loss came a tremendous and wonderful sense of freedom and exhilaration, a joyful anticipation of the future.

When Zack and Nora's son was born he felt at last that he was part of something he could hold on to with both hands as well as with his heart. With the new birth he felt a sense of closure for the family he had lost so long ago, when his childhood abruptly ended, and for the unborn child of whose existence he hadn't even known. He felt his future was in his new family, and it was his future as much as his destiny. It all at last felt real and genuine, it was all in place and it was finally true.

The Jesus Horse

He remembered Star's words, wondering if they had maybe been real words after all.

"No one is lucky enough to see the results of all that he has done."

Perhaps not. Perhaps Zack would never see all the results. But he had seen enough to know it was good.

Zack and Nora graduated on the same day. James and Lena and their children sat with Nora's parents, taking turns holding baby Jameson. After the ceremony they had all gone to dinner at a local Italian restaurant. Dinner had been light and enjoyable and everyone laughed. No one spoke of the past, from that point forward, only the future mattered.

Zack and Nora were due in Lexington Kentucky in two weeks to start work. Zack had eagerly accepted a job with the United States Dressage Foundation and would be administering services on-call for shows throughout the region. After going through the different rotations required by the veterinary program he had quickly firmed up his long-standing decision to specialize in equine preventive and sports injury medicine.

Nora eventually found a job with a Lexington veterinary clinic, with flexible hours to allow her to be with Jameson while Zack was away, and the soon-to-arrive newest addition to their family, baby Paul.

Zack loved his job. It took him away from home, but not for long, and it always brought him back with the strong desire to be there. It was as close to heaven as he thought he could be on earth. He loved the smells of the horses, he loved the activity in the barns, he treasured each experience and everything that had brought him to this place in his life.

And it was through work that Zack found himself face-to-face with a part of his past he hadn't forgotten, but had long ago put behind him.

He was on-call at the 2009 USDF show in Lexington at the Kentucky Horse Park. Because of several injuries in earlier events, his schedule had allowed him to see only the end of the Grand Prix level finals. He didn't recognize the name of the horse or the farm, but there was something about the rider that was familiar.

It was easy to find the right barn. It was easy to gain access. Perseus. Gold Springs Farm. Ridden by Mia Reed.

She was busy wrapping the big horse's front legs when Zack stopped at the stall gate. He didn't want to startle her or the horse, but she sensed he was there. He knew she didn't recognize him, at first. And when she did, he could see she was glad, and then concerned. Why would he of all people be standing outside that particular stall unless he had come looking for her?

"I thought it was you." Seems like we've both come a long way."

"Stella. You have Stella. How is she?"

Zack shook his head. He explained how he had changed her name to Star, and ended up selling her for tuition. He told her he had graduated from veterinary school, he told her about Nora and Jameson and Paul. Mia told him about Peter and Noel. She told him how she had ended up at Gold Springs Farm. She was sorry to hear he had sold Stella, but she understood, you have to accommodate what life demands. She told him how often she still thought of Stella, or Star. She told him how in a way she didn't think she would ever fully understand that her old horse had given her the strength, the vision, the words, to move on with her life.

Zack knew exactly what she meant.

Charlene

It had taken her a year to find the right person, but Charlene snagged a urologist with a condo on St. Charles Avenue in New Orleans. He was a nice man. She knew he would make a good husband. They met in downtown Austin at the 1816 Bar in the Driskill Hotel on Brazos.

Charlene had been at a networking meeting at the Starbucks across the street on Congress Avenue. A few of the group members had decided to have a drink afterwards. Dr. Dick, whose real name was Calhoun Ulysses Lee Dickenstein, was in town for a medical meeting at St. David's Hospital. He was drawn to Charlene's big Texas looks, accent, white teeth, and dynamic personality. She was drawn to the initials that followed his name, M.D.

After a year of visiting back and forth from city to city and state to state, they were quietly married in Las Vegas. For their own reasons, neither wanted a big wedding. Charlene suspected Dr. Dick was just too shy but the real truth was that he didn't want her to see how few friends he had. For Charlene, she just wanted it done.

Charlene packed up and without looking back at anything in her life, moved to New Orleans.

She tended to come on a little too strong for what uptown New Orleans society circles were used to, a little pushy and overly assertive, a little too Texas, and the other doctors' wives didn't trust her or her motives. Charlene thought it was because they were afraid their husbands would find her more attractive than they, but she had no designs on other men. It would never have occurred to her that she stood out in that group like a Halloween costume at a formal affair.

She and Dr. Dick were compatible. They went about their own ways, meeting in the dining room for breakfast and dinner when their schedules allowed. While not very exciting, their sex life was at least consistent.

Because she no longer had to work at a job or career she cared nothing about, Charlene joined a health club where she worked out every day, volunteered at the Delgado Museum of Art, and shopped. She filled her days, but Dr. Dick sometimes wondered with what. He wished she had some direction. He wondered if she was happy, if she was at least content, if she was at all satisfied with the life she had chosen, or was it one she had settled for. He didn't really want the answers to all the questions, but at the same time, he didn't want the questions to come between them. It wasn't something to brood over, but it was something to consider.

He didn't particularly want children. They took so much energy, but if they had a child, he thought it might keep Charlene home more, give her a focus.

She didn't really want children either. They took attention and time. As it turned out, even had they both wanted a family, Charlene wasn't able. She sometimes looked back and wondered if it was because of the abortion her senior year in high school. But it didn't bother her that much. It's the way it was. It was done. It was the past.

Charlene had been surprised to hear from Zack. She was more surprised to learn he was married. She didn't know why that was. Of course he should get married if that's what he wanted, she just never had pictured him with anyone but her.

There were times she thought of Zack, of the laughter, the fights, the talks, the companionship they had shared for most of their lives. There were parts of it all she missed. What she had now was different. It was sufficient, it was enough, but then again, it was far from how she might have scripted her life.

Dr. Dick had worried when Charlene seemed a little down after talking with Zack. Why shouldn't her old boyfriend get married? Why did that bother her? He knew it was just jealousy, and not real jealousy at that which bothered him. Not suspicion, not distrust. If he were honest he would probably call it envy.

But Charlene was more restless than usual. Her husband thought again that she needed purpose. She needed motivation, some inspiration, something that would define and drive her days.

Charlene was thinking the same thing. She just didn't know what it was, or how to say it. And then she did. It hit her flat in the face. She had always acted on impulses. Why not?

She'd always wanted to be Miss America. It had been her dream. Well, that wasn't going to happen. But she had experience. Anyone who had been through the pageants she had, held the titles she had held, anyone who had spent four years as the Hays County Pork Chop Queen, had experience.

She had a "Mrs." in front of her name now. A prestigious "Mrs." So, why not Mrs. Louisiana? Why not Mrs. America? If Zack could become a veterinarian just because a stupid horse said he could, she didn't see any reason why she couldn't be who she wanted to be. It wasn't spite, she told herself. It was who she was destined and driven to be.

At first, Charlene didn't share her new plan with her husband. She wasn't sure what his reaction would be. She met with the pageant coordinator. She met all the requirements for participation. She had a successful marriage, and did volunteer work in the community. She could easily be a role model for other married women, just as she knew in her heart of hearts, she had been to so many grateful teenagers for all those many years before. And, she knew she was still attractive, had a competitive drive, and knew how to work a pageant for all it was worth.

Talent was an optional event. Charlene still had her flaming batons. She would need to practice, but what a spectacular show she would stage. At her age, it would be even more stunning. She knew she would ace the private interview with the judges. She could easily speak about concerns and points of interest, and she could just as easily answer questions about charities, particular causes and activities or events that brought personal joy to her life, even if she had to fabricate or stretch the truth just a little. Everybody did it. She knew what the judges were looking for and she had it all and then some, personality, poise, beauty, speaking ability and overall appeal.

When Charlene told Dr. Dick of her plan it was already a done deal. She had mentally and emotionally committed, paid her fees and dusted off her batons. For him, there was first the wonder and astonishment that she would even have thought of such a thing, then the question as to why such an idea, and finally a total and overwhelming sense of pride, in her and himself. Was he, plain old Dr. Dick the urologist, in fact married to the next Mrs. Louisiana?

As fate or destiny would determine, yes.

Charlene spent the next year fulfilling her Mrs. Louisiana duties and commitments. Then it was on to Mrs. America International.

Charlene had never been happier. She had never felt more fulfilled. She loved the camaraderie, the pageantry. For the first time in her life she felt she belonged, really belonged, in this one exact spot in time. She was sure she had met her destiny. Thank God for Zack and his talking horse.

That night, in Palm Springs, when her name was announced as she walked across the stage to accept her crown and make the traditional, customary walk down the runway, one of her first thoughts was of Zack. It had all been such a long time ago. They had held such big dreams. Funny how much things change. How dreams adjust and transform to what life makes of them. Why is that? What makes that happen?

She wondered if Zack was watching the pageant? But at the same time, she realized she didn't really care. Dr. Dick was. He was right there, right in front, cheering her on. He was proud of her. He was proud of himself because of her. He was happy for her. He believed in her. Wasn't that enough?

Bubba

When Bubba was born he was all chrome. He was as full of himself as domestic foals come. He had a wild eye and an untamed spirit. Strength, character, temperament, personality, and will, he had it all. Back then his name had been Golden Bullet. His owners were afraid he would live up to the name as well as the disposition that went with it.

He surprised them all. He adapted well to training. He treated each new event as a personal challenge, and he was more than willing to prove it. The thing was, he didn't see anything in it for him, not in the proving of anything. It's how he had been since the day he was born, and no one had convinced him there was any other way to be. He would do what was asked, when he wanted to. When he wasn't in the mood, he was difficult and uncooperative. He was a horse unto himself.

When he was three, Golden Bullet was sold to a man who knew his horses. Understood horses, understood and appreciated what motivated them. Bullet, as he was usually called, had met his match. It was his new job to actually work cattle. And it was work. The new ranch was almost 3,000 acres. Cattle and hay production were its lifeblood.

Bullet learned to cut, he learned to spin and slide, he instinctively knew how to pull against the rope, and found that he enjoyed it. He was good at it. So good, that his new owner decided to do a little rodeoing with his new horse.

They made a great team, and little by little, moved up in the rodeo circuit.

When he was ten, Bullet found himself in the National Rodeo Finals in Las Vegas. The lights, the noise, the activity were like a tonic. He had never felt so alive, so full of promise, and didn't think it possible to feel such a thing again.

He was right. Sliding into a stop, pulling the rope tight, feeling the flexor tendons in both rear legs tear, it was over as fast as it began.

Some people, maybe most, would have put him down. He might or might not be rideable again, he most certainly wouldn't work cattle again and rodeo was out. Treatment would be expensive and time consuming. The outcome wouldn't be clearly known for over a year.

Bullet's owner chose to give him a chance. He knew his horse was stubborn enough to heal. And he did.

Eight months later the owner's grown daughter, visiting for the summer, rode the Golden Bullet in the Fourth of July parade through town. Shimmering with one of his fancy silvered rodeo trophy saddles and matching headstall, combed, brushed and oiled till he gleamed like golden butter, he was again on top and the center of attention. People pointed, wanted to reach out and touch him, watched in admiration as he passed. He responded in kind, prancing, tossing his head, jigging and jogging.

But the daughter went home, back to New York when summer was over. There was no one left who rode just for the pleasure of it. Riding on the ranch meant work, and the Bullet wouldn't do that work again. Then again, within three years, neither would anyone else.

The ranch sold to a development corporation for what the press reported as "an undisclosed amount." It was to become a subdivision. No more cattle, no more hay and no more horses. Just little square houses lined up on little square lots, driveways and garages in front, patios and fenced-in square grass plots in back.

Golden Bullet was given to friends for their grandchildren to ride when they visited.

They were nice enough children, they didn't kick, they didn't tug, they mostly just sat, and it didn't make for a very exciting life. He was their only horse, and he was lonely. After a few years, even the grandchildren lost interest.

His next home was a summer riding camp. He was their most requested horse, at first. But one-by-one the happy campers discovered it was almost impossible to stay on his back. It wasn't so much that he bucked them off, he just made it hard for them to stay on. A twist here, a sharp turn there, just a little hop, a low-hanging branch. Bullet wasn't any happier there, than they were with him.

At the end of the summer he was not one of the horses they wanted to board over the winter until the camp filled up again the following year. He was a liability.

When the camp couldn't pay one of its carpenters who did odd jobs keeping up the improvements, it offered to pay him with a horse. The carpenter knew nothing of horses, but he liked Golden Bullet's looks. Problem solved. Problem created.

And that's how, when he was eighteen years old, the once celebrated Golden Bullet came to be standing in a great boggy puddle of mud.

He was too thin. The outline of every rib was visible. He wasn't happy. He was generally resigned, reconciled to what he had become. The haphazard fence wouldn't hold a goat, but a hot wire kept him standing there, all day, every day, in the mud. The hay was old, moldy, and tasted like rotten grass clippings. There was no shelter. Two other horses shared the pen with him, and they were worse off than he. Day in, day out, it was what it was, but it wasn't what had been expected. It wasn't who he was, and it wasn't the way things should be. But it was.

His name was just Bullet now, but he didn't look or feel the part. The new owner put an ad in the local paper. Bullet was for sale. There was nothing to do, nowhere to go, and the only exercise he ever got was when someone showed up to see if they wanted him. Then he had to put up with all kinds of abuse from people who had no business being on a horse.

Did a 250-pound woman with rowel spurs who bounced up and down and stabbed him in the side with each step, jerking his mouth because she couldn't hold her hands steady, have any idea what that did to him? Did she know what kind of mood that put him in? Did she really wonder why she found herself sitting in the middle of the road?

Great, he thought when he saw the new people approach. More people to prod, poke, and probably want to ride. And they had kids.

The new people took him out of the muddy pen, tied him to a tree, and began brushing. The woman and two children brushed and combed, the man talked to his owner.

"I don't know nothin' about him," said the owner. "Just as how he's real gentle. Got him from a kid's camp. I got eight hunnerd in him, and that's what I'll take."

When he was clean, sure enough, out came the saddle. The woman saddled him, led him around, watching him, then mounted. She had soft hands. She nudged him forward with her knees and calves. No kicking.

After the ride, the brushes came back out. And then, back to the mud.

But the next day the vet came, drew blood, listened to his heart and lungs, looked at his feet.

And the next day after that, the woman and man came back, without the children, with a trailer. Bullet had another new home. Almost immediately he became "Bubba." He much preferred Bullet as a name, but maybe Bubba was who he had become. It seemed to be a term of endearment, and anyway, he didn't have much of a say in it. He had a new life and a new companion. What's in a name?

He took one look at his new friend, saw all at the same time a remote, worldly and yet unearthly look in her eyes he hadn't seen before in other horses, and knew without a doubt that he was in for an interesting, if not remarkable experience. In a way, a horse sense sort of way, he knew he was looking at his destiny.

Six years later, when Bubba was 84 in human years, he knew it for a fact.

Pidge & Midge

Does anyone really care about what happens to pigeons that move on? Eventually Pidge and Midge did. There was still grain on the ground daily under Bubba's feeder, but it wasn't enough to hold their pigeon-dove interests. They had a mission to fulfill, and other calls to answer. Lots of olive leaves, or cedar branches to carry. Lots of peace to make, or at least the effort to make it so. After all, they were only pigeons. They were only messengers. They could only do so much. Someone had to be around to receive the message. Someone had to be willing and open to what they brought and then be willing to do something with it. Someone had to listen, and listen with all their senses. There was need.

Pidge and Midge opted for Sixth Street in Austin. With an interesting nightlife, lots of other pigeons and plenty of food sources on the street, they found new opportunities for spreading what they had learned from Star-Baby to a large homeless population. Pidge and Midge were a little surprised to find just how accepting many of them were to what they had to say. Yet, in a way it made sense. If anyone had time to listen to pigeons, it was people who had nowhere else to go.

And the pigeons and homeless souls spent so much time, moving from corner to corner, place to place together that it really wasn't unexpected for them to find something in common. Many of those on the street had been without a vision, without hope or solutions for so long that they had forgotten how to look, and at the same time, how to see.

Whether because of poverty, addiction, mental illness, domestic violence, or something else, for them it seemed there was no opportunity left. The stress of becoming homeless caused many of their population to resort to odd or extreme behaviors. There was nothing to be discovered, nothing to embrace, it seemed there was nothing leftover at all for them.

Even though they knew they were pigeons, Pidge and Midge, with a little encouragement from Star-Baby, considered themselves to be at least dove-like, and as such saw themselves as symbols of hope and peace and even a little optimism. It wasn't that much of a stretch for those without anything to look to them for a sprig of hope, just a glimmer of something solid. A little solid ground, a little footing could go a long way.

Pidge and Midge knew many homeless people walked a razor edge between flight and suicide. Many escaped abusive relationships only to find themselves in a more slowly burning fire. But, by then it was too late and too many simply found themselves stuck, with no hand held out, nothing to save them but perhaps each other. And therein lay the solution.

"Two by two" suggested Pidge and Midge. "There's support in numbers. Put your heads together. Ideas are free. It's what you do with them that counts. Besides, what do you have to lose? Think of the freedom in that."

"Street smarts," said Pidge. "That's a commodity."

"Go with what you know," said Midge. "It's your own, individual perspective, unlike any other. But perhaps as good as any other if you just give it a push. You're not alone."

"Think about what you have to say that no one else can say," suggested Pidge. There it was. A voice at last.

And two by two and more, that's exactly what happened. Ideas were born, plans were formed, that lost gleam of hope became a spark, and then a flash, and then a blaze.

Sometimes just a little spark hits like a bolt. And then too, sometimes a little luck can strike like lightning.

"Voice on the Street" was born. Paper and pens were borrowed from shelters. Those who knew even a little about computers were allowed time in shelters that provided these amenities to those willing to use them. They were not in great demand, so there was plenty of time to set their own hours. In return, the homeless performed odd jobs and chores at the shelters they frequented. Sometimes they were able to barter for clean clothes, toiletries for keeping clean and presentable, sometimes for a giftcard for more supplies.

Over several months, enough stories had been told, written and organized, and they were ready. They divided into groups—sales, presentation, distribution, and creation of new material. Those appointed to sales began to take the idea of their *"Voice on the Street"* newspaper to local merchants to sell adds. Those in charge of presentation took their creation to local and city newspapers and printers for free or donated printing services. Those in charge of distribution visited supermarkets, book stores, churches and synagogues for distribution outlets.

They were working, and they were working for themselves. Almost immediately, they began to see the rewards of their labor. Feelings of self worth skyrocketed. Other newspapers wrote stories about their paper. *"Voice on the Street"* grew, and added to its staff. It was a snowball rolling downhill, rolling fast.

Personal and private donations as well as equipment began arriving. The word was spreading. The path out of social exclusion was emerging. People wanted to help, and that help became a hand-up instead of a hand-out.

"Star-baby would be pleased," thought Pidge and Midge.

It didn't happen immediately. In fact, no one noticed until the first freeze. The shelters didn't fill up. By the next freeze three weeks later, they were only half full. Where had so many homeless people gone? The answer wasn't rocket science. It was a simple idea that resulted in providing a springboard out of homelessness, despair and alienation.

Of course, no one asked Pidge or Midge, after all, who would think to ask a pigeon anything, but Pidge and Midge knew. They had seen it happen before. They knew where it started and they knew where it would end. Where the human spirit was concerned, they knew what just a little hope could do.

Part Five

August, 2012

The Jesus Horse, Stella, Star, Star-baby

History tells us a story. Our countries tell us a story. Our parents and families tell us a story. The Bible tells us a story. Mine is a different story, but it is a story rooted in faith. Some roots run deep. Some roots are shallow and grow and spread near the surface while others grow deep before branching out. These are the taproots, the main roots of a primary root system. They grow straight downward, allowing smaller lateral, secondary roots to form, which in turn produce even smaller tertiary lateral roots. It is this system that provides the nourishment that life demands.

"Behold! I tell you a mystery. We shall not all sleep, but we shall all be changed, in a moment, in the twinkling of an eye, at the last trumpet."

This is a prophecy, and as far as I can be sure, it has something to do with me. Whether it is foresight or insight, or is maybe just a vision, I'm pretty sure it is a warning.

I can't say with certainty what for me, this new world, is all about, why I'm here, or exactly what I'm supposed to do. I don't really have clear directions. I'm just a horse, for God's sake. Yet here I am, preparing mine and your minds for action. It seems I am here in part to set your hope fully on the grace that will be brought and revealed to you at a time to come. I, no more than you, know when that time will be.

I do know the world today is frightful, exciting, full of good and evil, corruption and honesty. There are signs of a complete disregard for life, for the earth, the oceans and the heavens that sustain life. There are examples of self-serving manipulation, and at the same time, examples of the greatest care and love and boundless joy. Do you have any idea how big, how complex, how entirely intricate this makes this world? It's absolutely an elaborate pattern.

And of the future?

Will there be divine intervention, Illumination of Conscience? Will all the light in the heavens be extinguished? Will the sign of the cross be seen in the sky as darkness takes over the earth? These are questions without answers. They are questions of how you define faith. It's not the same belief, not the same definition, and it's not made with the same conviction for each person. Because, see, we are all of us, every one of us, different. That difference can create huge barriers, but it can also bring us together in a simultaneous, collective action. Our differences, combined can be powerful.

Picture the eye of a hurricane. A calm, a silence in the midst of a great, global storm. It isn't calm for long, as the storm rages through. That eye is a reprieve, and its time is short.

Do you remember the bible story of the thief breaking into a house? The homeowner responded that had he known the time of the thief's arrival, he would have made adequate preparations for the event. What kind of preparations exactly would he have made? Another prophecy perhaps, but it never hurts to be ready, to be prepared, for the best and the worst that can happen.

I do know that early in my life I felt things, knew things that other horses don't know or feel. This knowledge continued to build and grow throughout my life. Sometimes it surprised me. Sometimes it scared me. Often, mostly, I wasn't sure what to do with it.

I didn't know if anyone was listening, if anyone even cared, or what they would do with what I tried to say. Whether I enlightened anyone, whether or not it stuck, whether or not my message spread, may not be the point. That point may be as simple as, I did what I could, putting it out there, leaving it with those in need to take from it what they most needed.

Life isn't easy, and contrary to popular belief, it's not a mystery that needs a solution. Life is a path, a direction. There's a lot more to it than a sense of security, which it seems is in high demand here on this earth. And, it's pretty obvious that security, sanctuary, doesn't come about easily, and it absolutely doesn't come with easy answers.

You might not want to hear this, but life doesn't end with all the answers suddenly made clear, anymore than that security everyone is after comes with them, the answers. But the questions, now that's a different story. If people only knew that it's the questions they should be after. No matter how hard you try, no matter how determined you are, I hate to tell you, it won't be enough. Not everything can be figured out. Sometimes it just all comes down to a little trust, a little faith.

However you define faith, as trust, loyalty, devotion or belief, it may well be the gate swinging wide, of salvation. Yet, by itself alone, faith is dead. Without a reference point, even faith has no path.

I will tell you this, when your faith grows, it will see you through to the end. Faith is not an option, it is not a choice of greatest convenience and is not a part-time activity. No one tells you how to live by faith. It can't be taught, it can't be borrowed and returned, it can't be bought and sold. It's invisible, and it's not, not when you know how to look.

When your faith is greater than the situation that calls for faith, you have grown into faith. It will move you in the direction, as a conduit on the path you choose to follow and forge.

I loved all the people, all the beings I came to know. Maybe I didn't really like them all, that's a lot to ask, even of me, but I did love them. I wanted them to be better people, do better things, make better choices. I wanted their lives to have meaning. I wanted to see them giving completely, giving gently, receiving in turn.

Mia

Mia was the first human I ever saw. I knew immediately that she was troubled. I didn't know by what, but I could see in her eyes that joy was missing. That pure joy that drives the heart and soul. There was no bliss. I know I surprised her, maybe scared her a little. I seem to have that effect on people. Yet, she had been happy to see me. I had finally arrived.

She was a good person, in a hard place to be. She didn't know it yet, but after things would fall apart, she would put them back together with a then unknown grace. And she would flourish in a newfound life she could have never imagined.

What most people don't know, until it is too late, is that life isn't about the lines and compartments we create, living inside those lines and never moving beyond them. Too much time is spent on defining boundaries, and too little on challenging those same boundaries. There's a careful balance, and with it a tipping point between despair and hope, and to her credit and spirit, Mia learned to see what she felt were failures as stepping stones. Those steps carried her far, into a future she would have thought impossible, yet it was one she could fully embrace.

After the disaster with Richard, and the loss of everything she had loved, she loved again, recognizing that if she didn't hunt out, find and seize every opportunity to grab happiness she might never get the chance again.

Mountains and prairies, ups and downs, good and bad, in the end, it really is a question of balance. It's a matter of recognizing what is most needed, when and where.

Mia's heart was open, and when your heart is open, it is amazing what can find a home there. Love. Love must be nurtured and cultivated, it must be allowed to develop and choose its own time. Love can't be taken, but is given as a great gift, willingly and freely, without strings, without judgment, without conditions.

It grows, you know. As a vine or a tree with those wide-spreading tendrils and roots, love grows.

And when it's gone, you'll recognize, too late, what a gift it was. You'll want it back and when you have it, you will fight like hell to keep it.

Richard

Unfortunately for Richard he really never had a clue. He had been born to wealthy parents who were as distant as if they had not even been there. He was an only child, and would have liked to have a brother or sister, someone to share his loneliness with. He was cared for by what seemed to be an endless progression of nannies until he was old enough to be sent away to school.

It was at school that Richard finally began to learn there were other people in the world that mattered, and it took him awhile to learn how to interact with these other people. It's not that he was particularly selfish or self-centered, it was more that he didn't know what relationships were, what was involved, what should be given and what there was to take. He had never been nurtured, and had no idea how to nurture or cherish or support anyone else. He had nothing to treasure. But that would change.

Richard had somehow managed to develop a self-deprecating sense of humor, despite never having much of a role model to develop anything. He knew of his short-comings. He knew he had work to do. He just didn't know how or why, to go about it.

On his sixteenth birthday his parents gave him a new car, a BMW convertible. It was delivered to his dorm with a note from the dealer.

He drove it home for spring break, but his parents, without notice, had gone on a cruise. He was alone, and it was a familiar place to be.

Richard graduated, attended college, graduated again and went to work. Work was something he understood. It was about value, about what you did, about what you created, what you were capable of doing with who you were. He was good at this part of his life. And, he knew it.

Then he met Mia. She was everything he wasn't. He had hoped she would round him out, that there were parts of her missing in him he could make his own. Unfortunately, that's not how souls develop.

Richard's soul took more time than many. His was a bumpy ride, and when it settled, he was in a new, unchartered for him, but agreeable place. The circle was not quite complete, but he was pulled back from the edge. He had been given a gift, a gift of the heart, and finally knew it.

Zach

Zach was a good man. He learned the meaning of pain, and the frailty of life at an early age. He also learned that life does go on. It takes on a life of its own.

He could have chosen different paths at any point in life, and they would have taken him different places. Some of those places would have been better than others, some were the places he would most certainly look back on with regret.

It's not that Zach never thought of the past as free of regret, but he knew it was not a place to dwell. Still, it had pointed him to the future many times, to its own solution.

Zach had dreams of his future, of success and happiness, and at the same time he knew well that success and happiness were not the same. He also knew not all dreams come true, some you can finesse, some you can fool, but when just one dream is realized, really and truly is true, there is always that element of surprise. Maybe there shouldn't be. Maybe that's what keeps us from following our dreams.

We all have rational senses that tell us dreams are dreams and have nothing to do with promises or how our lives will turn out, they are dreams that have nothing to do with the future. Yet Zach had the idea, the suspicion that there might be more to dreams, to the senses that connect us all, in ways unimaginable.

One promises another, one becomes another, circles become complete. Zach lived a dream, his dream and made it a reality. It stretched outward, it swallowed others, it embraced them all, and it became the future he had dreamed.

Backhoe Operator, Jim Bob

Jim Bob was a character. He was private, bull-headed, loud and soft, all at the same time. He was much more than he appeared to be.

Jim Bob never forgot his encounter at the stockyard in Amarillo, and he never forgot the voice he heard. He kept it all inside, but it was how he reached out to others from that day forward that revealed his changed spirit. It was with fortitude and a greater purpose that he was determined to live the rest of his life.

There were things about himself that he could never explain to anyone. They were things he didn't understand on any level, things he couldn't talk about because he didn't know how to think about them or what they meant. It was when he tried to think about them, about what his strengths might be, about what he was meant to be and do, that the details became scary.

That was when the "old" Jim Bob peeked through. When he was scared, he knew he wasn't the person he wanted to be. When he was scared, he wasn't a person anyone would want to be. When he was scared, he felt he was being swallowed by everything around him, and people ended up emotionally hurt, psychologically cut-off.

That Jim Bob had been gone a long time, but every once in a while, he tiptoed back in. Tina had seen it happen. She thought it was hardest for her husband and left it to him to work out, which he usually did sooner rather than later. Afterwards, only the remnants remained, a destruction that bordered on dry hunger. And, then it was over, it was gone again.

When he let himself, Jim Bob thought of these episodes as dream-like events, taking place in a surreal world. It's as if his life became a dream, and the moment when he awakened, that exact moment would be death. So simple, to him, so simple that in its simplicity it had to be true. When you died, that's when you woke up. That was heaven. But he didn't know how to share any of this. He didn't want to bring anymore unhappiness into his world, or into the lives of his family than might already exist.

He knew well-enough that it wasn't only evil and immorality that made people unhappy, it was also uncertainty, confusion and misunderstanding. It was where he had spent the first part of his life, with the failure to recognize the very simple truth that other people are as real as you.

Charlene

The world is full of persona, each a unique being, each with their own definitions, their own demons and their own means of grace. Charlene was a handful. In her own scattered way she was looking for a version of herself she could live with, trying on one persona and discarding it for another, much as one might slip on a favorite pair of shoes, before changing into a pair that made more of a statement, rounding out the entire impression.

What was it that Charlene wanted so badly that she could barely live in her own skin without it? What was that thing that was always just out of her reach?

It's true, that's a broad question and it's almost always about what we don't already have. Are they the things that bring us pleasure, or reward. Are they things that stimulate us? Do they make life more meaningful? Maybe we want them just because we don't have them and someone else does?

Here's where Charlene had it wrong. She had never given a thought to regret. How do you know how you will feel about something you've never experienced? And how will you feel about what you give up to experience it? Then what? Charlene was after what she thought she wanted, had to have, but had no guarantee that it would put her life right. The not having, made her want it even more. It was a lot like forbidden fruit.

I felt for Charlene. She was like so many others, and at the same time, felt she was someone more special, more deserving. She wanted the spotlight, the fame, the title, because she thought someone else wanted it, and that made her want it still more. And, as soon as she thought she might not be successful in her quest, she rebelled. She just reacted, the only way she knew how, proving that yes, she could get what she wanted. And, she did.

The unanswered, and unasked question is, where did she go from there? What did she take away and what did she leave behind?

If you asked Charlene, she would not have been able to give you a response. She could just never let go. And always, for the rest of her life, she would have a sense of loss, a place where she had never been but was waiting for, finally, remembering it had already happened. Finally understanding what could never be again.

It always goes back to that one thing, the true wealth, the true north, the true purpose of each of us, that is the impact we have on the lives of others. No matter how big, how small, how noted you are, until you give to others, you are engaged in a never-ending pursuit of emptiness.

Gretchen

Gretchen could never bring herself to tell anyone, but for as long as she could remember she had felt as if she had a guardian angel watching after her.

She knew she didn't always make the right choices, and she seldom made them for the right reasons. Yet, she always seemed to move forward. It was as if she was doing battle with herself, wanting what she didn't have, maybe wanting it with the wrong motives, but wanting it all the same.

That's when the guardian angel would guide her, often to a different place, with a different outcome, and Gretchen would find herself where she wanted to be.

That guardian angel of Gretchen's was one of love. Love is more than the most powerful emotion we can feel. It is love that gives us power, and at the same time, gives power to everything in the entire universe, whether we acknowledge that power or not. It is a single thread, and it ties our fabric together in a triumphant bond, one human being to another. It is love that creates the incredible tapestry of human life and emotion. And it is love that transcends time.

Love, with its nurturing and healing effect touches us all in different ways, yet ways that are ultimately and invariably the same. When given, it returns.

In Richard, Gretchen hadn't looked for love. She was exploring other pursuits of gratification. At the time she didn't know what she wanted, only that the want was there. A craving for something so far indefinable. It was a vague and obscure quest, and one she had taken on without much thought to where it could lead.

She had learned how tangled life can become, how knotted and twisted outcomes can be, and how hidden those paths might be buried. But, she knew they were there.

Gretchen believed in her heart in her guardian angel, but never understood all that the angel brought. She never knew the ties from one world to the next, or how they simultaneously guided her from one place, one experience to another. Yet they did.

There is a thin veil between our experiences and our worlds. But that thin veil reveals an incredible thickness between belief and need.

Gretchen found what she needed, what she had never explored or known, and the answer was as much a surprise as a solution. She just hadn't known where to look. She hadn't learned how.

She also learned that it is never too late. Never too late to start over, never too late to try again, never too late to grab happiness, in whatever form it might present itself. It might be unexpected, it might be unpredicted, and it might be unrecognizable, at first, but like her guardian angel, it was there when she needed and least expected it.

Bubba

Bubba wondered if, thought probably so, was actually pretty much convinced that he had seen a miracle. More than that, he had played a part in its making.

He couldn't explain it, even if he had been able to communicate it. But, that's the thing about miracles, no explanation is really necessary. They just are.

It was all much bigger than Bubba knew, than he could even grasp, but he knew he had already been a part of it, and he knew too that he would always be a part. It was the best of who he was or had ever been, and he was proud of the role he played.

Bubba's life had been saved after his rodeo accident, and he was pretty sure when it had been saved again through an ad in the paper, that Star-baby had a hand in it. Those incidents may or may not have been miracles, they may have been nothing more than chance. But Bubba believed that something much greater than chance had been at work in his life. And he wasn't the only one. Not by a long shot.

It was about changing behavior from the inside out. Fixing it up. Fixing what is broken, fixing what needs to be fixed. Doing the best you can. And then doing a little more.

From Star-baby, Bubba came to believe that not all miracles encountered deal with life and death, that some actually save lives from unforeseen outcomes, save lives so that other lives might be changed. The wonder of miracles is that they are hidden, yet lives are still, maybe subtly, quietly, even imperceptibly altered, beyond the reach of human action.

Such faint distinctions, barely noticeable acts, are sometimes all it takes to save a life from self-destruction, whether self-induced or from unacknowledged and even astonishing, surprising places. Bubba had seen this himself. Miracles happen, and are sometimes not ever even noticed, the outcome becoming part of the miracle.

Really, he knew well enough that impossible things happen, that over time you encounter more and more meaningful coincidences in life, more synchronicities, all accelerating to the point you feel you are experiencing the miraculous. And, maybe we are.

He knew it would be a challenge, and that the challenge, really, was in how to bridge the ever-widening gap between what was ancient biblical text, however one chose to interpret it, hiding in its pages the wonder of miracles, and today's world of internet, indulgence and instant gratification. How does one go about even attempting to bridge that divide?

Through Star-baby, Bubba had seen how. It had to do with belief.

"Belief is a wise wager. If you gain you gain all, if you lose, you lose nothing."

What was Star-baby doing quoting a seventeenth century philosopher?

She wasn't finished.

"It's more than belief, you know. Belief alone doesn't take it far enough. It's a call to action, for all of us, a conviction that must be recognized that we can do more than passively acknowledge miracles exist. It's time to gather them in.
That's the mystery of the world, hiding behind our lives, yet shining so brightly we can't even look."

Bubba came to acknowledge that the far-reaching effects of miracles go much farther than anyone can realize. Maybe that's why they happen more often than we ever know.

Pidge and Midge

Now, Pidge and Midge, they were a surprise. Even I like surprises, now and then. It took no time at all to find out what they were up to and why and how they ended up in my barn.

I know, it's been pointed out already, that Noah had white doves, not grey and brown pigeons. But, I'm willing to bend a little too, do what I ask of others, and birds are birds, goodwill is goodwill and hope is hope.

It's true, the world could use a few more sprigs of hope these days. It doesn't take much, just a little sprig, like an olive leaf in a dove's, or pigeon's beak.

We already know the Noah story addresses the issue of survival of the whole human race. That's a pretty big story. What was it about Noah? So the story goes, when the earth was in peril, when all was threatened, Noah said nothing, he quietly acted. He acted on his beliefs. When the flood was finally over it is said, he left the ark, celebrating with an all-night drunk. What does that make him? Human? The definition doesn't matter, he made a difference when a solution was needed.

The Noah story points out that when life is in danger, those who regard themselves as reasonably decent people can make a difference. We are all obligated to act.

The story of Noah is an amazing tale of one person's willingness to seem like an old fool in a world intent on destroying itself. Today I hope we wouldn't call that crazy or foolish. I hope we might call it courageous.

Back to Pidge and Midge and doves and sprigs of hope. Noah may have been just a crazy old man, but if you believe the story, his faith may have saved the world through his crazy actions. And when that dove came back, can't you just imagine it? That bird just standing there, a freshly plucked olive leaf in its mouth, standing there on its pink legs, heart beating fast from the flight, offering not craziness but irrepressible hope. Offering just that one little sprig of hope to a chaotic world on the brink of survival.

Peel the layers of the story way back, and it's not hard to visualize Pidge and Midge offering hope to homeless people. Why not? There is an urgency to acting in time when the issue is human survival.

The Woman / Narrator

Of all my people, it was The Woman I most connected with. I remember when she first saw me. She hadn't known what to expect. She wanted a horse. She saw a horse. She saw a dream realized. And, she saw right through me.

That was the first spark, the first hint that something powerful, and out of her control was about to happen. We both felt it, in our souls and spirits. I knew then how it would end, but that wasn't something to be shared. It would not be recognized.

Souls and spirits may or may not be the same thing. That's an argument as old as time and one I'm not really all that interested in. They're both essential, fundamental to life fully lived. Think of the minefield your life would be without either of them.

If you believe the soul is indeed the essence of humanity's being, if it is who we are, the spirit is then that aspect of humanity that creates connections. When your spirit rejoices and your soul is joyful the future is illuminated with clarity and brilliance.

That's what it was with The Woman and her connection with me. If the soul is the seat of our emotions, will, and moral actions, and the spirit is our highest self, having them in agreement with each other is central to a life well lived.

When your soul longs for happiness, experiences sadness, jealousy and loneliness, it can be tugged apart. It's your spirit that pulls you back together. That Woman had a lot of spirit, she had to have had to put up with me.

I remember the day she came out to feed, much like every other day when it started, then suddenly twisting into a new version of itself. It was when she said, "I know who you are. I'm just not sure why you're here. I mean not just here, but here in this particular barn. Why here?"

"Why not here?" I said. Then, I think I scared her when I quoted Revelations.

Then I saw heaven opened, and behold, a white horse! The one sitting on it is called Faithful and True, and in righteousness he judges and makes war. His eyes are like a flame of fire, and on his head are many crowns, and he has a name written that no one knows but himself. He is clothed in a robe dipped in blood, and the name by which he is called is The Word of God. And the armies of heaven, arrayed in fine linen, white and pure, were following him on white horses.

I thought it would help explain the why of the here and now. The second coming. That was a lesson learned. Too much, is more often than not, worse than not enough.

It is said that death is the ultimate statistic, that one out of one people will die. Because this physical world is bound within time and space we often make the mistake of thinking that death is the ultimate end, the exact moment when something ceases to exist. But death, and its companions goes beyond physical death. And the people it leaves behind are changed people. They become the second death.

I knew how my story would end. I worried for the people, souls and spirits I left behind. I hoped, but wasn't at all sure that faith would be enough to carry them forward. The world, and all our behaviors in the world are complex. Hope isn't always enough. And faith is more than the opposite of doubt. And it's faith that will ultimately, that must, see us through.

The Woman had faith. She recognized its role, and what it could do, that belief with strong conviction, a certainty in something for which there may be no tangible proof, that complete trust in or devotion to.

Today's faith has become a twisted and misused word. It's what is used when reasons begin to build up against what you think you ought to believe. For far too many, and for their own reasons, faith has become religious wishful thinking. It shouldn't come as a great surprise that people raise their eyebrows when 'faith' is mentioned. Is it strange that they seem to prefer what seems like reason over insanity?

The Woman accepted what she saw, what she knew to be. At the same time, she couldn't explain it, couldn't really understand it, yet appreciated that comprehension wasn't what was required. She saw, she waited, she questioned. Without the assurance of things hoped for, the conviction of things not seen, it wasn't a bold leap-in-the-dark faith, but rather the kind of faith that results in doing. And that she did.

Part Six

August 2012

Narrator

And so what is it that we long to find with such an intensity and passion that we never stop searching, and with such fervor it consumes us if we let it? Maybe that's not such a bad thing, yet at the same time, do we, do any of us, really appreciate or acknowledge, or even recognize exactly what it is we hope to find? Do we? And, how many of us can truly say we've done everything we can do to find it? After all, where in fact is life going? Who can say? And ultimately, who has the right to say it to anyone else?

I consider myself fortunate. Sure, there have been bumps, actual ravines, roadblocks, obstacles and detours, moments of the greatest joy and of the deepest sadness. Life is big. And, those three small words hold a world of hope.

I told myself it was good where it counted, where it was important, in all the ways that truly mattered. So what really was financial success on the great scale of life? What's a little hardship along the way, a little adversity, a fraying thread? Hell, a fraying rope? What really does smoothness, or fairness, or even contentment have to do with it? We all know you come into life with nothing, and you leave the same way. But there's a lot that happens in between. Those spaces between the notes are as much a part of the music as the notes themselves. According to Star-baby, we live by the rhythm of our stories through the cadence of connections.

"Stories live transformed, changed and re-told by signs not made and words not spoken."

Star's words. And all of it leaves traces and trails, many that go places never imagined, but land there all the same, some with direction, some without. I've heard it said, "It's not the answers you should be after—it's asking the right questions." Those questions lead to many more places than do a few answers. Some are unexpected yet truly wonderful surprises. Isn't life supposed to be full of surprises?

I believe that none of us will ever find all the answers we're after, but if we're lucky, we'll find solutions to our most important questions. For me, when those answers and solutions began peeking through the shadows, working their way through the tunnels, I didn't know what to do with them. They touched elements of my life I didn't know how to explain. Fundamentals and essentials I couldn't logically address, but then, there they were. My life was affected, no doubt. But, mine was not the only one.

Here's the funny thing. It seemed all of a sudden as if I had a lot of answers, at least they seemed to be answers, some to unasked and deeply buried questions. And still, even with what appeared to be a complete glut of answers, I was really at a loss.

And just exactly where did those answers unexpectedly come from?

What was it about now, about an isolated moment, a detached place in time? I had heard the words in my head. Words from my horse. Really. I knew those answers came from the Lovely and Talented, from her very presence. But who could I tell? Who would believe? A horse, my horse, told me this so I know it to be true? Talk about a stretch of either, or combination of, imagination, faith, or belief.

But I knew it was. I knew it was its own truth and I knew it went further still. It already had. It was on its way. And, in its way, it would touch the world. It would spread through the world, person to person, soul to soul, essence to essence. It was that big. And it was that simple. It was all a fine thing, a thing of scale, with a sweeping glance, just a fleeting moment, that touched us all. A thing that had to happen, and would now happen with still unforeseen and far-reaching consequences for all of us. Maybe because that's the way it should be, had to be, and finally was.

Horses live deep in your soul. Their largeness, the fluidity of movement, at the same time their independence and dependence, their smell, the mix of hay and manure, a sweetness that belongs and at the same time doesn't. Anyone who has ever said, "there's just something about a horse," has known exactly what is meant.

As soon as I knew what a soul was, I knew, I felt in my being instinctively, that mine was destined to be shared with a horse. I wasn't sure how, when or in exactly what way that bond would come about, but I always knew it would be a special relationship, someday. And so it has been.

Through all of it, good, bad, fragile and tenuous I somehow knew. And, I knew in my heart that it was Star-Baby all-along. She was my dream, not a human dream, not really a definable dream, yet my dream come true, and as such she provided the hope, expectation and strength to see that realizing one's dreams truly is possible. In the course of the way of life, from end to end, and first to last, without her heart and spirit and character, it would not have happened as it did. Much of it, may not have happened at all.

At the outset, I said I didn't know how I came to be telling this story or accounting for this sequence of events— and I still don't. But, I know a lot more than when I first started, mostly because I've lived it. I know there are others who are more qualified to recognize and identify the consequences of all that has occurred, who are able to read between the lines and clearly see what it all means. But then again, I'm pretty sure it's nothing new and nothing singular. It, every bit of it, is all out there for each of us, to see, interpret for ourselves, internalize and move forward, and move on, and on until the motion itself takes on a life all its own. Maybe that's why it might mean more coming from a person with no exceptional credentials. It really is, exactly what it is.

I don't know when it really started and I don't know how or when it all will end, or even if there is a true end, but I do know now that it doesn't really matter. Not anymore. It seems as if we really are all here, doing what we do, living a cosmic drama in a cosmic universe on a cosmic scale. Eyes wide with a plan. Don't we all have a plan? And in it all, how important is one little action, one little success, one little, or even one big, mistake?

According to Star-Baby, the importance of it all is impossible to judge. It just is, and it, every single action, holds the potential to be so big and so far-reaching you can never see the distance all at once.

According to Star-Baby, life, real life, is full of realities, not metaphors. We tend to feel the need to explain the truth, and we grope after a metaphor to illuminate and make clear that truth.

It's true that metaphors tell a great story. It's also hard, if not impossible to live up to them. And, still, no matter what you do, or plan, or intend, it all moves on. It all moves forward. Over and over again. And when hearts and minds are moved, they can change the world. This is the difference between reality and metaphor, this is what realities do.

But, and this is the hard part, the part that must be bridged to move forward, there is a great chasm between those exposed metaphors that lead us to reality, often a reality that is far beyond our ability to separate into manageable actions, and the very human metaphors that bring the reality within our focus. There is great disparity between those revealed metaphors that bring flawed and broken human beings as close as is possible to the truth, and the human metaphors that bring those same beings to a certainty they can fully hold.

I always knew horses were special. I knew it. I know it still today. I'm pretty sure that horses come as close to a human metaphor as you can get. For me, it wasn't about riding, or grooming, or the cost of hay, feed, tack or veterinary bills. It's about getting what you ask, and need of life, and more often than not what you get is at the same time no more but no less.

It's that simple, yet its simplicity is complex. It's an intricate and elegant and connected place to be, all at the same time. But that's my world, horses and more, metaphors and more, life and more, the future, and beyond.

That's my world as I know it and embrace it. But then, for each of us, our worlds are different, and yet, they are exactly the same. We all live in our own and connected worlds. The connections run deep, deeper than on a personal level we can ever know. Each connection reflects every change in the connected chain that forms our lives. And, at the same time, that's what holds it all together.

It's all we have, these chains, bonds, ties, and we, all of us, have to do more than consider the links in those chains, we have to question the whys. What links us together? We have to ask, we have to insist, we have to demand. We have to live as though life depends on it. And, more often than not, it does.

That's where horses, you might say the metaphor of horses, come in. They rely on you, and you on them. They are big. They are strong. They are power. Lives become connected and forever dependent, in ways that go far beyond words and definitions, beyond horses and humans.

It finally does come down to what lives deepest within your soul.

The answers, the magic, the gifts, don't come about with bright bursts of light, bands of angels, blaring trumpets and the swinging open wide of heavenly gates. It's not about miracles, dumbfounded awe, or astounding wonder. It's about who we are, and who we want to be. It's about how we go about being. It's about what we did yesterday, and today. What we will do tomorrow, and the tomorrow after that. It's about how we do it, every bit of it, from the commonplace, mind-numbing and tedious, the most ordinary and mundane, to the most excellent and brilliant parts each of us can offer.

It's about our bright spots, our ability to do our best for ourselves, and at the same time to understand the needs and wishes of others, all of the many others struggling and juggling through lives much like our own. No doubt about it, it is a struggle, but it is also life lived to the fullest. That is our challenge, our charge, and it may well be our destiny.

And yet, all at the same time, the hardest thing to acknowledge is that it's not necessarily the brilliance, or the brutality, the splendid kindness or most vicious cruelty of what life is capable of, but rather the hesitant apprehension that it will, in its own time, in its own way, happen. And that's where we come in, with all our baggage, all our faults, all our fears, and all our dreams. It's where we blindly and boldly or even timidly make a stand, and then make a difference as best we can.

That's what it is. Each and every bit. All of it. Bridging the gap of understanding. Looking at ways to recognize other patterns and thoughts, because without that comprehension, without that capacity, all we have is unhappiness, unfulfilled dreams and lost expectations on all sides.

It may sound fanatic, and yes, it may sound frenetic and chaotic, but I know this at least is true. It may or may not be a happy truth, depending upon how you choose to view it, but it is huge, offering nothing you can hide behind.

Part Seven

December, 2012

Star-Baby was excited. She hated storms, was terrified of storms, and the air had been strongly laced with the fresh ozone of pending rain all night. It was after midnight, the wind from the north raged and howled, unrelenting. As the storm built, the dark of night grew darker still. The darkness was heavy. It was so intense as to almost suck the breath from the air itself.

Star-Baby pawed hard at the ground, loosening the heavily-packed caliche clay. She snorted, turning northward to breathe in the direction of the wind. Her wide, soft nostrils expanded and then contracted. Her mane blew back from her neck in great white waves. With tail high she began a slow gallop around the corral. Her hoofbeats drummed the hard earth as she picked up speed. Bubba, standing in his stall, looking out at the approaching storm, let out a short, shrill whinny. Warning, encouragement, or something else? Star responded.

"It's alright, Bubba. It's as it is supposed to be. No one takes it from me, but I lay it down of my own accord. I have authority to lay it down and authority to take it up again. So will be the coming of the Son of Man."

Another prophesy. Lightening from the east, shining as far as the west lit the corral with an unearthly color, bolts striking close enough that a pungent, almost cordite-like scent filled the air. Star-Baby gathered speed and with almost imperceptible effort, left the ground, easily clearing the corral fence in one great, bordering on frantic, leap.

At the exact same moment in time that she became airborne, lightening struck again, this time with devilish, or heavenly accuracy, and Star-Baby continued her head-long acceleration in a weightless, and now timeless, forever timeless silence, the love for those who had loved her driving her on.

And she was gone, as simply as that, as finite as that, to an undefined space, to the place where her future, maybe our future, waited.

Narrator

Where does the difference lie between devastation and realization? Between awareness and faith? That difference creates a big gap but not so big there isn't a big answer.

Was she really here? Was she who I came to believe she was, or was she just another horse? Does it matter? I think it does, in a way much larger than I can begin to acknowledge or answer.

I know she changed my life. I know she changed other lives. Through each connection, each encounter, she offered the strength, courage, and even motivation, to keep going when it sometimes seemed there was little reason to go on. And, isn't that reason enough? Isn't that what we're supposed to do?

Paths had been crossed, destinies touched, perhaps bent, perhaps nudged, but forever altered. Yet each time, with each whisper of contact, something of the essence lingered long after, passing from soul to soul, person to person, generation to generation, on and on and on, like a vague glimmer of something elusive and intangible but real, lost and at the same time found or waiting to be found, to hold forever yet lose again in an instant, something to define, but so obscure as to be not quite definable. Really, at its core, how else to define this life we all pursue so relentlessly?

And of all she left, through it all or because of it all, her greatest gift would always be in the ever-expanding, never-ending love she left behind. Love never really dies. It grows and develops, from person to person, life to life. From a seed to an orchard, to a forest, to a jungle, and then, to a clearing in the center of it all. It is the noise of the heart.

It was this final gift that in and of only itself would lead one, should one choose to look, to find, treasure and embrace truth, hope and love, in a world that never promised any of this, in a world that never promised anything, in a world that is as it is and as it has always been, leaving it up to each of us to seek and take what we ultimately need most from it, and in the end, leaving behind our own legacies of love, faith and hope.

And, that's about it. The last thing Star-baby said to me is also one of the stickiest things she ever said.

"Words are easy. It's the actions they incite that are hard. But, it's the actions that make a difference. And, we can all make a difference.

"We work all our lives to be who we become. And, it's who we become that determines what becomes of us."

That's a lot to shoulder, a lot to bear. It's a lot to take on faith. Then again, it depends on how we live our lives, day in, day out, what we do and how we do it. In a great big way, we're all part of the same story. And, we're all our own stories in the end. It seems the challenge is to make it a good one, to make it one that matters.

Acknowledgements

The world is a big place, and virtually, it gets bigger daily. The consequences truly are amazing. The information at our *everyday* disposal is growing at a breathtaking rate. From the beginning of civilization to 2003, the world accumulated 5 exabytes of data. That's 5 billion gigabytes. That's 18 zeroes following the number 1. That's the equivalent of all the words ever spoken by mankind.

Today, we generate that same amount of data every two days. And, these numbers change and grow daily. This is so much data that to put it into perspective, a full 90 percent of all the data in the world has been generated over the last two years.

Just think of the stories in all that information.

While writing this book I was continually amazed by what I don't know, and what I do know, what I know just a little about, and what I know just a little enough about to be dangerous. It all has to come from somewhere, and I thank my parents, Glen and Linda West for giving me the freedom and opportunities to explore all my sometimes crazy and off-beat endeavors and ideas many years ago. Look what they have turned into. With each new direction and undertaking my mother would say, "you have another bee in your bonnet." Guess so. Thank God for those bees.

I'm still exploring. I realize nothing happens in a vacuum, and the writing of this novel is no exception. It has taken time, faith and belief. A lot of each.

To my wonderful daughters, Alexandra and Whitney, thank you for being my earliest readers—and for liking it. To Fred Stern, how did you ever find the typo on the back cover in just the first glance? I'm so glad you did. To Daniel Becker, I'm sorry Alex wouldn't let you read the draft—you can read it now.

And to my husband Jay, thank you for not pulling out your red pen, thank you for the support, and thank you for being you. You are the love of my life.

I would also like to pay tribute to the numerous books and articles that helped in my research for this book. The world is indeed full of wondrous information. I am in awe, and happy to have been able to learn from it.

For the cover photo, thank you Alexandra West Becker.

www.ingramcontent.com/pod-product-compliance
Lightning Source LLC
Chambersburg PA
CBHW021038130626
46552CB00005B/1913